£ 1-50

CW01095728

May We Have A Word?

An Anthology of Short Stories and Poetry

'Write Now'

authorHOUSE®

AuthorHouse™ UK Ltd.
500 Avebury Boulevard
Central Milton Keynes, MK9 2BE
www.authorhouse.co.uk
Phone: 08001974150

First published by AuthorHouse 12/31/2007

ISBN: 978-1-4343-3864-8 (sc)

*Printed in the United States of America
Bloomington, Indiana*

This book is printed on acid-free paper.

Dedication

This book is dedicated to the memory of Chris Lammas who died in February 2007. She was a much-loved member of 'Write Now,' and never ceased to amaze us with her grace, kindness, and courage. The following tribute was written by Pat Higgins, another writer from the Group.

Christine

From across the room I was aware of her, a pained expression on her face, grey she looked. "I'm not in any pain," she said during the coffee break. "Losing my hair has meant more to me than I expected; this wig is driving me mad today, I just want to pull it off and throw it."

"Cancer has pulled the rug from under my feet." (Her words, not mine.)

I like Christine; she feels life. What I know of her is very little really. She sings, music is in her soul. She is strong in her views, but I see a fragility in her. The need of us all to be held secure in someone's arms.

"I love women," she once said to me. "I love men too, but women have a great strength to face all things." These words really had an impact on me. I have always felt a need to emerge from within myself, searching for that strong woman.

Pat Higgins

Contents

Introduction

The Authors of this Anthology are all members of 'Write now.' This Writing Group meets at Soken House, a Community Centre situated in Frinton.

The Group was formed when an Adult Education class in Creative Writing was discontinued some years back. The disenfranchised students decided to continue meeting and writing, and to pay for the hire once a week of their old room. --- And the rest, as they say, is history. Other writers have joined the Group since, but the majority are still the ex-students.

There is a strong link to the ever growing Frinton Literary Festival; It was students of the Creative Writing Class in collaboration with their Tutor John Gladwell who conceived the idea, and who worked tirelessly to bring it to fruition. As we finalise this book the Festival, whose Patron is Poet Laureate Professor Andrew Motion, is entering its sixth successful year, and although the managing committee has seen faces come and go some of the originators are still involved (including two of the authors contained herein!) we wish them well. The Festival does sterling work in encouraging people of all ages to read books, and to take up the pen themselves, and we urge all who read this book to support it.

Acknowledgements.

'Write Now' would like to thank Bill Lammas for all his support and encouragement, and for his unique illustrations. Bill also helped Roma Butcher to produce the cover photos.

Thanks are also due to Tendring Council for their assistance under the Small Grants Scheme, and to Councillors Iris Johnson and Robert Bucke who encouraged us to apply.

Farlowe Chicane

I parked my 'Olds' and crossed the sidewalk to Joey's Bar. The sweat running down my back had nothing to do with the LA heat and everything to do with what might greet me inside. The note back at my PI's office on ninth said three o'clock: I was half an hour early. I had no idea who I was meeting; the signature was just 'L'. I knew that a lot of people in here were gonna be pissed to see *me*; the bill-fold inside the note was a jerk in this direction. An overhead prop fan was doin' its best to push the smoke fumes back into the choking darkness of the bar, and the silence at my entrance made the atmosphere even more friendly. I could tell Joey was pleased to see me when he spat on the floor behind the long counter as he eyeballed me whilst wiping a glass with the end of his vest, his huge tattooed arms flexing. I was the centre of attention as I split the customers and reached the bar.

"Joey" I said in greeting.

"Farlowe" he grunted. "Didn't expect to see you again."

I looked around. Every guy looked like a Marlborough ad, only less friendly.

"Guess a beer on the house is pushin' it?" Joey's silence was answer enough.

"Ok, give me a short" I said, and laid a twenty out.

The darkness, if possible, got darker, and I felt rather than saw a menace behind me. Turning, I faced a set of crooked, chewing teeth unmistakably owned by Fists Fellatio, brother of a two-bit dealer I had put away on my last visit here. All six foot three of him, and that could have been width, he had obviously gone up in the world, as he was flanked by two more Marlborough men. Heavies ain't cheap these days.

"Howya doin' Fists? It's an honour to see someone so ugly so early in the day."

Fists was the only one chewing in the place, and my remark stopped his hobby for a tad. He looked me down and down --- him bein' four inches taller --- then spat the contents of his mouth directly onto my new loafers, my right one. The chewed spearmint landed and stuck over my big toe.

"You ain't welcome in here -- Gumshoe."

I saw the rest of his mouth as he laughed, joined by his pals. I figured now was as good a time as any, as if Fists and company didn't get me, the smoke would. I canned him with a right and saw some teeth go; then sidestepped the guy on the left, connecting with his ear. -- Painful. Two down and I was doing well, in for the break, when the room went bright white, followed by the lights going out --- maybe they were mine, but I was past caring.

The blackness was receding and I was still down, but this wasn't no floo. Everything but my head was comfortable. A kind of sight returned, and I saw I was on a bed. Things were lookin' up and somehow I registered that the gum had been removed from my shoe. I felt that my hands weren't tied, and gingerly touched the back of my head. If it was walnut season I had grown a winner. The room was bright; evening sunlight slanting through expensive shades. Wherever I was this wasn't Joey's on Fourth Street, and I could even smell the sea. Real pictures broke up the floral walls, but the most surprising aspect of the room was the angel at the end of the bed. It had to be an angel; they don't make 'em like this in LA. She was tall and slim and had on a beautiful face framed by orangey blonde hair down to her square tailored shoulders. The rim of her hat couldn't hide her live green eyes or the sensuous red lips, both pointing in my direction. I couldn't see the legs, but if it was made as a package, then they'd be more than saleable.

"How's the head Mr Chicane?" she purred. The voice was East Coast and washed over me like a spa bath. This dame was class and plenty.

"I been slugged before. It ain't so bad. Who was the electrician?"

"I must apologise Mr Chicane, I turned your lights out as a matter of, shall we say, self-preservation. Yours of course."

"Mighty kind of you Miss ------ or can I just call you L?"

"Frontall. Lara Frontall."

"I'm sure you do Miss ----- Frontall. My head tells me it might not be a good idea, but the rest of my body tells me it's gonna be good to get aquainted with you."

"Oh I was taught that I should always be a pleasure to meet Mr Chicane."

Boy, this room was getting hot!

By Simon Butcher

Hidden Treasure

Tyres scrunching in the gravel we drove reluctantly away from the thatched cottage. Alice and I stopped the car and took a last look at the chocolate box picture; honey coloured thatch, wisteria tumbling down over leaded windows, it slumbered in the sunshine as it had done for centuries.

Surprisingly it had been an enjoyable week. We had both shed many tears, but there had been laughter too. I had lost my Peter and Alice her Ted within three months of each other. We had all been friends for so many years; Peter and I always left our beloved King Charles spaniel Sandy with Alice and Ted when we went on holiday, and we returned the favour by having Buster, their Heinz 57 mongrel. Both couples had been so lucky over the years, travelling the world, but since losing our respective partners Alice and I had lost heart in exotic locations, so a cottage holiday in Somerset with our pets had seemed like a good idea.

We bought a local paper and found local craft and garden centres to visit, enjoyed a film at the Village Hall, and went to the theatre in one of the local towns. We took the grateful dogs for long invigorating walks in the glorious countryside and ate delicious home-cooked meals at any number of country pubs. Today had been the perfect end to our holiday. It was a wonderful day; after a light shower the sun had shone from a duck-egg blue sky. I stood in the garden, closed my eyes and breathed deeply, the smell of wet grass mingling with the scent of flowers delighting my senses. On our last walk through the village we stumbled on a church fete. The man on the gate said that Buster and Sandy were welcome so in we went.

The first things we bought were toys for our pets. We wandered round, and ended up at the Hoop-la stall. That was fun, and we actually won a goldfish! Then we went and watched the children dancing around the maypole. Alice nudged me. "Let's buy some jam and marmalade to take home. And those scones look nice!" As we wandered in the direction of the jam stall, we passed a young man selling knick-knacks. He was wearing a mad jester's hat, and was capering about. He turned to us.

"Roll up, roll up, roll up, it's the end of the day ladies, just a few bargains left. Come along my dears, just £1 a box." His bells jingled as he danced all around us, his eyes pleading, "Take pity on me!" He pulled a tragic face. "My wife will kill me if I take this lot home!"

We rummaged among the boxes, and nestled at the bottom of one of them, among the soft toys and odd cups and a tatty old framed print, was a pretty china trinket box. On the lid there was a depiction of an elephant standing on his head. Now, I was immediately interested in this because my little granddaughter collects elephant memorabilia.

"How much for this?"

"Sorry dear, you'll have to take the box. One pound please."

We walked back through leafy lanes high with cow parsley and buttercups, pleased with our bargains.

Several weeks later my three grandsons came to ask for jumble for the Scouts.

We spent a pleasant couple of hours searching the house and garage, putting on old hats and fooling around. The box of oddments from the church fete was added to the pile, and I caught sight of the picture. I said to the boys, "I rather like that frame, I think I'll keep it."

Alice gave me a lovely surprise for my birthday. It was a tapestry of our holiday cottage. She must have worked on it for months! The hollyhocks, roses, delphiniums and foxgloves were a riot of colour. I gave her a hug.

"I've got a frame that might suit it, come on, let's see if it fits." We gently pulled back the hessian and carefully took out the dirty old print. Imagine our surprise when we found another picture wedged between the two layers!

"That's not a print," said Alice thoughtfully. I snorted.

"Whatever it is, I don't like it. It's ugly! It looks like a child's drawing." As I stood looking at it, a vague memory started to nag at the back of my mind. "You know, I'm sure I've seen something like this before. I'll probably be wasting my time, but next time I go into town, I think I'll take it in to Golds.

"Yeah, yeah, yeah," mocked Alice. "It could be a Matisse or a Renoir! You should be so lucky!"

Mr Sims was a tall silver-haired gentleman, he was immaculately dressed and had a rich cultured voice. He was ages looking at the painting, so Alice and I wandered around the gallery, looking at all the beautiful works of art and pulling comic faces at each other. Then he called out to me.

"How did you acquire this?"

"I bought it."

"How long ago?"

"Oh, quite recently."

"Mmmm, and may I ask how much you paid for it?"

"Certainly, you may ask, but I prefer not to answer that question."

"Of course madam, that is your prerogative." He stroked the painting with his long tapered fingers. "In my opinion this should be insured for three million pounds."

I felt faint, the room was spinning. Alice's voice seemed to be a long way off.

"Gracious! Goodness gracious! Well I never!"

"And if you were thinking of selling," Mr Sims continued, "I would advise that a painting of this importance should be handled by Christies. You may expect at auction in the region of two and a half to three million." My legs started to shake as I stood up and took the painting from him.

Covering it with the two pillowcases I had wrapped it in, I said breathlessly, "Thank you so much Mr Sims. I'll let you know my decision. In the meantime I would appreciate complete confidentiality." He nodded and shook my damp hand. On the way back to the car I clutched the painting in front of me.

"I think I need something stronger than tea Alice, and please not a word to anyone about this. I've got some thinking to do." Alice promised, and we agreed to refer to my secret as 'It.'

Two nights later I awoke from a deep sleep and crept downstairs to find a young man coming out of the dining room.

"Where is it Mrs?" he growled.

"What do you want?"

"You know!" He edged nearer. I could smell tobacco and beer on his breath, and a knife flashed in his hand. I felt the tip of it on my throat."The painting! Where is it?" The next day I was still shaking as I phoned Alice.

"It's gone Alice," I told her. "A courier came this morning to take it to London. I had the most horrendous nightmare, and having 'It' in the house was making me feel ill. I'm living in a state of fear and excitement and I want peace of mind."

Christies had been very interested when I told them about Mr Sim's opinion. They seemed to think it was an early work of the artist. They confirmed that it was legit, so at least I knew that I wouldn't be arrested for handling stolen goods!

Summer's here again. Alice, Buster, Sandy and I are back at the cottage. Last month our local paper printed a picture of the new annexe for the Toddler's Play Group, and the new Scout Hall, both built as a result of an anonymous donation. My children and grandchildren have had dream holidays. I told them that I had an insurance policy that had matured. Well, in a way, it was true! I just massaged the figures a bit. *My* treat was to buy our holiday cottage so that we can visit whenever we like. So, as we chink our glasses together and sip our chilled champagne, Alice says,

"Let's drink to good old 'It.' Cheers! Down the hatch! Bottoms up!" A bit later on, she whispers to me, "Let's get the local paper and see if there are any fetes on this week. That jam we bought was very tasty!"

By Valerie Woollcott

Granny Bank

*B*ottle Banks are everywhere. They take all sizes, shapes and colours of glass and jars. In other countries they are thinking of having Baby Banks, where you can abandon a child that is unwanted to give it another chance in life.

I think it would be a step in the right direction if there were a Granny Bank where you could deposit all the old folk that are surplus to requirements. This would relieve the Tax payer of pension costs, health care, and funding Nursing Homes for the 'oldies,' also reducing the burden placed upon families for looking after their old Mum and Dad.

When the time comes you could wheel them to the Granny Bank situated in the High Street or Supermarket concourse and simply post them through the slot. Once inside they fall onto a soft mattress; an Emmett style mechanical arm and large rubber suction cup on the end reaches out and places them on a conveyor belt onto the next stage. This would be to assess their mental ability. They would then be placed in an appropriate cubbyhole and colour-coded for future reference. A doctor examines them as to whether there are any bits and pieces useful to the Spare Parts Department. These parts would be sent to the Workshop for reconditioning. The surplus sent to their appropriate cubicles to await further arrangements. At this stage reasonably fit persons could be rehomed, or if they do not wish this they could be available for tea making.

Once reconditioning is complete, these parts would be sent to the Consultant section for distribution. The waiting list for parts is three months from the appointment time. Heart and kidney transplants take longer with a two-year wait. Persons of a more delicate constitution would be placed in a refrigerated unit to preserve what is left in good condition.

When processing is complete, previous owners are contacted to let them decide if they want them back in their renewed condition, if not they are forwarded to the recycling centre.

By Pamela Harris

Alas, Nowhere.

She walks among us
To be pitied, or scorned at
Through the cold wind and rain
She seeks shelter under
Draughty alleyways or canals
Where is she going?
Alas, nowhere.

Alone in the crowd
Picking out scraps of food from
Dustbins, her tatty clothes
Covering her weary body.
Some pass by her without a second
Glance. Others tinkling in her
Tin with a few coppers.
Where is she going?
Alas, nowhere.

Through the dead of night
When we sleep in our cosy beds
Her cigarette butts stuck to
Her chapped lips, she puffs away
Until sleep relieves all feelings of cold
Where is she going?
Alas, nowhere.

By Mary Ann Naicker

Flight Of The Wolf
Chapter One

The heart of Running Wolf was heavy. He knew his life was over. The Bluecoat soldiers would choke the breath from his body in a day or two, but in his mind he was already dead. He longed to join his beloved Moon Woman who had been taken from him so cruelly. The interminable banging and crashing from the scaffold being built on the parade ground outside the barred window was a constant reminder that Yunke Lo the bringer of death was waiting outside the door.

The constriction of the tiny cell was oppressive. If he stretched out his arms he could touch the wall on either side. It was dark and filthy, and he was constantly playing Peep-Bo with a large brown rat. No matter, he was Sioux, a Badface Oglala, a warrior. He would show these white-eyes nothing but dignity.

He was roused from his thoughts by the clank of the outer door opening. -- He saw from the slant of sunlight through the window that it was past noon, and he knew that he had a visitor. -- It would be the Bluecoat holy man, the smooth cheeked one. His Jailer, whom the Indians called He Who Limps, thrust his key in the lock.

"It's the Padre to see ya Injun. -- You take care you behave yourself, hear?"

Lieutenant Joseph Hanrahan, the Regimental Chaplain, entered the cell, clutching his well-worn bible. As he sat gingerly on the end of the narrow cot the Jailer locked the cell door.

"Just sing out when yer finished Padre." He limped back to the comfort of his wooden chair and the bottle of booze he kept in the desk drawer.

The tall Sioux gazed impassively at the smooth and earnest features of the young Lieutenant. There was a long, heavy silence. Finally Hanrahan spoke.

"Have you given any thought to what we talked about yesterday my son?"

Running Wolf had been taught English at the Reservation School and he spoke it perfectly, but he instinctively embellished his speech with the graceful gestures of Sioux sign language.

"I have given thought to many things Captain." He called all Bluecoats Captain, unless he was fighting them.

"Then you will repent your sin and ask for forgiveness?" The young man's face was shining with faith.

"Should I repent for killing the Coyote? -- The dog who raped my daughter and murdered my wife?"

"Why do you call him that? You should show respect for the dead. -- His name was Sergeant Buchanan."

"On the Reservation he was known as The Coyote. His heart was as black as his beard and he slunk on his belly in the dark. Like all Coyotes he only attacked those who couldn't fight back."

"But don't you understand, he was a white man, a Christian. And besides, his fellow soldiers have said on oath that the girl was willing, and that he shot her mother in self defence when she came at him with a knife."

In a quiet voice Running Wolf asked, "Do you believe them Captain?"

The Lieutenant said nothing, but the blood rushed to his face. The Indian continued. "No, in Indian law a child molester cannot be permitted to live. And death must be avenged. -- It is our way. I will not apologise for respecting the law of my people."

Hanrahan sighed. -- "I had hoped you would give up your pagan beliefs and accept the one true God."

"I am sorry Captain. I cannot forget the teaching of my people. -- You should know that death holds no fear for me. But, when Yunke Lo comes he will not permit me to pass through Wanagi Yata, the gathering place of the souls. And it is only from there that I may join my Moon Woman in the Hunting Ground in the sky. You will bury my body in your White-eyes grave and my soul will be trapped in earth."

The Lieutenant listened intently as Running Wolf went on to describe how Sioux Indians built their platforms for the dead on holy ground so that the body would face the open sky. The Shaman would say prayers to the God Wakan Tanka and the soul would fly straight to Wanagi Yata. Chiefs and the bravest warriors would be burned on their platforms and their souls would ascend in the smoke. His words were so sincere, and his distress so evident that Hanrahan was almost moved to tears. He stood up and put his hand on the red man's shoulder.

"I'm sorry Running Wolf. -- I cannot arrange a Sioux funeral for you. -- Army regulations would not permit it. -- But I will see that there is a grave marker with your name on it. I know that your daughter Star is staying with her Grandfather. -- I will see that she is allowed to visit the grave, and perhaps say an Indian prayer." He went to the door. "Jailer! I'm ready to leave!"

As the footsteps faded along the corridor Running Wolf stretched himself out on the cot and willed himself to dream of Moon Woman.

****

Chapter Two

$\mathcal{T}$he sentry was not much more than a boy. The beard that sprouted from his chin was mere fuzz. --- And with a boy's inexperience he was not concentrating on his job. With an Indian blanket thrown round his shoulders to keep out the dawn chill, he hunched over his rifle and daydreamed about the hot coffee brewing in the Guardhouse.

Eagle Claw took all this in as he climbed silently up the rawhide rope that he had thrown over one of the spikes at the top of the palisade. He and his four companions had crawled on their bellies under cover of darkness over the fifty-yard stretch of open ground between the wild sagebrush wilderness and the wall of the fort. Dressed only in their breechcloths and moccasins and carrying only their weapons they had daubed themselves with river mud and crawled with painstaking slowness to avoid detection. The slight breeze was blowing from the north so they had approached from the south. The stables and corral were situated at the north end of the fort, and their scent might have spooked the soldier's horses.

The Sioux warrior was now only ten feet from the boy, and as he took in the lad's youthfulness he felt a momentary pang of pity. Then he hardened his heart. All White-Eyes were his enemy. Moments later the boy was lying dead, sightless eyes gazing at the sky. Eagle Claw quickly stripped off the blanket, tunic and hat and put them on, taking care to tuck his braids inside. He stood up, and putting the rifle on his shoulder, he paced slowly along the platform, and then back. A low owl hoot brought the other braves swarming up the rope. Using sign language he instructed them to conceal the body, and then told them to take up their positions around the Parade Ground and wait.

****

Running Wolf had not slept. Visions of himself standing outside Wanagi Yata pleading with Yunke Lo to let him enter had denied him the mercy of sleep. In his vision he could see Moon Woman weeping and holding out her arms to him. -- As grey light seeped into the cell he threw off his fatigue with the blankets. After relieving himself in the canvas latrine bucket he knelt by the cot and prayed to Wakan Tanka.

The outer door clanked and he heard the dragging footsteps of He Who Limps. The Jailer balanced a tray on one hand, and was holding his Navy Dragoon Colt in the other. He brandished the pistol.

"Over against the wall, Injun! And no funny business!"

Obediently Running Wolf got to his feet and stood under the cell window. The Jailer put the tray down on the wooden bench outside the door, then he unlocked it and placed the tray on the end of the cot. The gun was trained on the Indian until the door had been relocked. He Who Limps snickered as he went back along the corridor.

"Enjoy yer breakfast Injun! It'll be yer last!"

A pleasant odour assailed Running Wolf's nostrils. For once his breakfast consisted of something other than mush. He examined the contents of the tray. There were two fried eggs, three strips of crispy bacon, hominy grits, and a couple of ladles full of beans. Two slices of buttered corn bread sat on a separate plate and there was a steaming mug of black coffee. He sighed. In spite of everything he felt his mouth water, and he attacked the meal with gusto.

As he wiped up the last of the bacon fat with the corn bread the familiar clank told him that his hour had come. Several men came down the corridor in sombre procession. Captain Hanrahan, dressed in cassock and surplice came first, carrying his bible and chanting a prayer. He was followed by He Who Limps, Colonel Jaeger the Fort Commandant, and two armed guards. Running Wolf stood up as the cell door was unlocked. The Chaplain continued to pray as the

Colonel formally intoned the charges against the Indian, and the sentence of the military court. As he finished he motioned to one of the guards, who drew a knife as he entered the cell. Running Wolf shied away, the rope was one thing; cold steel was something else.

"I'm sorry Running Wolf, they need to remove your braids." Hanrahan flushed. "It's to, -- you know, facilitate matters."

"Have you not shamed me enough? -- An Indian warrior's braids may only be removed if he is shown to be a coward or a traitor."

The Chaplain at least had respect for this courageous man, and he spoke urgently to the Commandant.

"Sir! I think we could show some mercy. -- Look, the braids are long enough to be tied together on top of his head."

Grudgingly Jaeger agreed, not out of mercy, but a desire to avoid any delay or unpleasantness. Finally, the procession, now including Running Wolf, walked back up the corridor.

****

Eagle Claw watched from the wooden ramparts as the death procession emerged from the prison block. Although his mind was racing with the rescue plan and what was yet to be done, he took in the proud demeanour of his friend. Over six foot, Running Wolf stood tall, his head was held high. The crude tying of his braids and the rough prison clothing could not disguise the noble bearing. As Running Wolf ascended the scaffold Eagle Claw emitted the cry of a Prairie Hawk as a signal to his comrades.

"Come Spotted Beaver," whispered Black Bull. And the two young braves descended the outer wall and silently made their way towards the corrals, making full use of available cover and shadow. Left Hand Hawk and Little Raven, dressed in the hats and tunics of two other unfortunate sentries took up their stolen rifles and settled into vantage points underneath the West Tower ---- They both ensured that they had a bullet ready in the breech.

Running Wolf shook his head as the blindfold was offered. His voice carried over the parade ground as he sang his death song. He wanted, no, he *needed* to perform the traditional dance of death; but his legs had been pinioned.

"Sioux Indian Running Wolf, you have been found guilty ----------------"

Once again the Colonel read aloud the indictment and the sentence. Then he nodded to the Executioner. As the latter raised the knotted noose over the Indian's head there came the shrill cry of a Prairie Hawk and a shot rang out. -- The Hangman was killed instantly. More shots came from the base of the tower and both the armed guards toppled from the scaffold.

Eagle Claw pulled out the fifteen foot board he had secreted on the rampart, and as he had calculated, it just reached the scaffold, forming a precarious bridge. Levelling his rifle and screaming a Sioux war cry he rushed across. Swiftly slicing through the rawhide that secured the prisoner's knees, he took Running Wolf by the arm and pushed him onto the narrow plank. His friend was not as sure-footed as he, so progress was slow, and bullets buzzed around their ears. Even as they crossed Eagle Claw was busy with the knife and the bonds fell away from Running Wolf's wrists. Left Hand Hawk and Little Raven had kept up a fusillade to cover their escape, and suddenly a neat hole appeared in the Chaplain's pristine white surplice. He sank slowly to the floor as blood seeped between his fingers.

From the corner of his eye Eagle Claw saw his two comrades moving back toward the palisade, and his heart lurched as he saw them both fall. -- He pushed Running Wolf to the place where the rope was secured, then he turned and fired at the pursuing soldiers as his friend descended.

Black Bull and Spotted Beaver were waiting below with six horses that they had taken from the corral, and as Eagle Claw threw himself onto the back of a huge Cavalry mount the four galloped off towards the wilderness. Five yards from the bush, which would give them much-needed cover, there was a groan and Spotted Beaver threw up his arms and tumbled to the ground. With pursuit hot on their heels the survivors had no choice but to continue the flight.

Running Wolf and his rescuers were thundering along side by side. As they crouched low and clung to their horses' necks he shouted across, "Moccasin Top?"

Eagle Claw nodded.

****

Chapter Three

Moccasin Top was a high plateau in the Black Hills; a secret place known only to the Sioux. It could not be seen from the trail below, and the opening to the track leading to it was obscured by thick brush. After so many years of living on the White- eyes Reservation few of the Oglala knew about it and even fewer ever went there. Senior braves like Running Wolf and Eagle Claw used it as a hideout, or simply a place to relax and find some peace and quiet.

After rising some fifteen hundred feet the narrow path opened onto a broad, wooded plateau. --- There was much game, one or two caves, and a freshwater spring. As they approached the secret opening Eagle Claw signalled a halt, and he dashed over to a tall cottonwood on the edge of the woods. He climbed nimbly to the fork of the tree, grabbed a bundle he had secreted there earlier, and returning swiftly he thrust this into Running Wolf's hands.

They dismounted, and leading the horses in single file, the three braves ducked under the lower branches and followed the narrow path upwards. The climb was tiring, the horses had to be bullied and cajoled, and as they reached the top around two hours later, Running Wolf was exhausted. Nonetheless his heart lifted as he took in the serenity of this holy place. --- They made their way to a shallow cave which was their usual camping place and tethered their mounts.

Running Wolf clasped the forearm of each of his companions in turn. -- He spoke warmly. "Woyuonihan my brothers. You have saved me from a shameful death. I am sad for our fallen comrades, but they died with honour."

"Aye Running Wolf, you may be sure that their bodies have been recovered for proper care."

Running Wolf untied his bundle and was overjoyed to see two parfleches, bags made out of buckskin, which contained his clothes. There were two breechcloths, beaded moccasins, a buckskin tunic, and his headband with a single eagle feather. -- The biggest prize of all was his own razor-sharp hunting knife, complete with its soft leather sheath. All his belongings had been lovingly decorated by his wife. --- He clasped Eagle Claw by his shoulders. "Thank you my friend."

For three days they did nothing. The fire was built with dry smokeless wood, and they rested and talked, leaving the camp only to hunt and fetch water. -- They reminisced about their heroes; Red Cloud, Crazy Horse, Dull Knife, Sitting Bull. Black Bull gazed into the embers.

"We are a spent force my friends. Once the Sioux were strong, our warriors were mighty. Pte the buffalo roamed our lands as plentiful as the stars in the sky. Now Pte is gone, and we shall soon follow." He spat into the fire. Running Wolf spoke next.

"They cannot take our honour. We fought for what was ours. We fought with honour, the White-eyes fought with treachery. We have laid down our arms but still they kill us. Even the good White-eyes like the smooth-cheeked captain pretend they do not see. We might just as well have continued to fight."

They talked for days of the great battles, the few victories, and the ignominious deaths of great men. An unarmed Crazy Horse had been stabbed with a bayonet while being held down, and Sitting Bull, harmless in his old age, had been cut down at Wounded Knee because the White-eyes were frightened of the Ghost Dance. Still, for the moment, they were safe.

There was a lookout point nearby, between two huge rocks on the edge of a tall bluff. One day Black Bull ran into the cave and beckoned the other two.

"Hopo! -- Hookahey! Let's go!" And he led the way to the lookout. "Look, they are swarming all over the prairie like ants!"

He was exaggerating, there were fifty or so soldiers on the trail below. They were moving slowly, but they were nowhere near the secret entrance. Black Bull grinned. "They couldn't find fish in a pond!"

The soldiers searched for several days, watched from above by the fugitives who took great delight in their ineptitude. Then one day they just seemed to give up, and they disappeared. The three companions were elated, and they reverted to the previous pattern of hunting, eating, sleeping, and reminiscing. --- Slowly, a plan started to take shape. If they rode west, travelling by night and hiding by day they would reach the Rocky Mountains. Using the highest mountain passes they would travel north to the land of the Grandmother. This was their name for Victorian Canada. They would disguise themselves as Crows, who were friendly with the Whites. Excitedly Running Wolf exclaimed, "Perhaps Star could come too! We shall have to risk going back to the Reservation for her!"

Alas, it was not to be. The very next morning a strange sound rose faintly to their ears. It was a metallic sound, and a hissing, like the sound of hot springs. They rushed over to the lookout and were astounded by what they saw below.

There were open wagons on the trail, filled with benches on which sat scores of armed Bluecoats. On a platform at the front of each wagon was what appeared to be a stove, belching steam and smoke. One of the soldiers sat at the front, holding a long steering rod. There were also some Cavalry riders milling around, but the horses shied away from the wagons.

"This is strange medicine," grunted Eagle Claw. "Where are the horses to pull them?"

They watched as the wagons made their way unerringly to the secret opening. Several whoops went up as it was found, and they saw some of the soldiers patting a tiny red man on the back. Black Bull spat.

"Little Dog!" he said contemptuously. -- "I might have known!"

Running Wolf stared down at the skinny old man sitting nervously among the soldiers.

"Little Dog?" he said incredulously. "I knew he was trading with the soldiers, but he is still a Badface. -- I did not think he would sink this low."

"He will sink even lower when I catch up with him," promised Eagle Claw.

They rushed back to the cave. Eagle Claw and Bull were frantically gathering their belongings and loading the horses. Running Wolf was strangely calm. -- He held up his hand. "My brothers, I cannot fight with you. My soul is weary. My reason for living has been taken from me. -- All I want now is an honourable death. -- Please help me."

And despite their fear his friends used their precious time to help Running Wolf build a wooden platform above the cave, lashing branches together, and piling brushwood upon them. Running Wolf knelt in prayer, and after a few minutes he climbed onto the platform and lay down. He put his hand on Eagle Claw's arm. "If you escape, go and find Star. Tell her I had an honourable death. If she wishes, take her to the land of the Grandmother. Goodbye my friend. Go with Wakan Tanka."

He lay back, and drew his hunting knife. He closed his eyes, and saw the beautiful face of Moon Woman. Her eyes seemed to say 'come to me my husband.' -- He relaxed, and exploring his throat with his free hand he located the jugular. With a sigh he drew the wicked blade across it. As his life blood soaked into the brushwood Eagle Claw intoned the Sioux death chant. Then he took out his special glass and held it up to Wi, the sun. Soon smoke rose from the brushwood, then a flame, and the soul of Running Wolf ascended to Wanagi Yata.

Claw leapt onto his horse. Brandishing his rifle he shouted to Black Bull,

"Hopo! Let's go!"

The End

By Bill Davies

Hatred.

'He's a bastard. I'll raise him as mine but remember, he's your bastard. There'll be no love from me.'

'William, for heaven's sake, it is not his fault and look, he's exactly like Adam as a new born.'

'He is not like Adam, he's not a Stone and he's not mine. I'll keep my word and I expect you, in turn, to keep yours and never mention his father's name again.'

'But he is a Stone.'

'He is not , woman' he bellowed, 'my young brother gave up any rights to this name years ago when he showed himself up as a con-man and an adulterer. Women all over the county - and now you. Take the tyke away from me, I've work to do.'

And so it began. William Stone worked to hide his shame. No- one knew the child Nathan was not his but he knew and his wife knew. He was already a wealthy man, landowner, property dealer and, of course, the home farm was his. He had bought his brother's share many years before when the younger man needed money to pay off gambling debts, or it may have been women. William didn't care, just to be rid of Leslie was all he craved. To have complete control of the land he loved was his right, he felt, and now that he was to be constantly reminded of his spoiled and lazy brother he swore to make this the biggest farm within a thousand miles.

He treated his wife with cold courtesy and the boy Nathan with contempt already knowing that he would grow into a mirror image of his loathsome father. He poured all his love into raising Adam in his own image, teaching him everything he knew about his beloved farm and the ever increasing boundaries, seldom noticing that though the boy was interested, he was not enthusiastic.

The boys were inseparable though Adam, three years older was not a natural leader and followed Nathan into all his schemes and adventures which more often than not ended in disaster. For which Nathan was always punished, Adam merely cautioned about his brother's wild ideas. Ideas which generally were meant to improve the farm about which Nathan was passionate but since his 'father' would never discuss farm matters with him, saying, 'Leave it boy, nothing to do with you', mistakes were made.

Adam's interest in art and design grew much to his father's disgust and his mother's pleasure. She helped him in every possible way, sending to the city for reference books and articles by interior decorators, magazines and brochures from leading galleries. For this William blamed his wife while Nathan watched it all with amusement.

Until the day he decided to dam a small stream diverting water to a far meadow with good grazing but dry ditches. He moved a few cows onto the meadow with their calves and returned to the farm, tired but bursting with news of his enterprise. He was a husky eighteen with no real interest outside of the farm.

He waited until they were all at the dining table. With the arrogance of seniority Adam sniggered 'You mean the flood meadow. Nice one, brother.'

William erupted. The fool boy had made a mistake and the ignorant cretin even found it funny. 'Look', he smiled, 'there's no sign of rain and I'll move them back tomorrow.'

'You think this farm is yours to do whatever you fancy? Well, you're wrong, boy it is not and it never will be, just remember that. It's Adam's and the fool ideas you kick around mean nothing. Do you hear that - nothing. From now on keep off the land and make yourself useful here in the fields.

Look after the hands and the horses, keep the stables clean and get behind a plough.'

'I'm not a dirt farmer, you pay Mexicans to work the fields. I'm your son.'

'No. you're not, you are your mother's bastard son, nothing at all to do with me. She went whoring around and you are the result, God help us. You may look like Adam but you are only a half brother. Alright' looking at his wife who as usual remained silent, 'I know I'm supposed to be quiet about it but I've had enough of him. Get out now, boy.'

Nathan was frozen and he wanted to hurt this man. 'Well, on the plus side I'm glad you are not my father. Don't ever again call my mother a whore, she's been a saint to put up with you. I suppose I should thank you for your patronage up to now. You must feel somewhat frustrated with your only son well in touch with his feminine side and not a bit interested in your life's work. At least you have a beautifully decorated farmhouse, a credit to Adam's good taste. What a pity you have no friends, no visitors, could it be you're a mite too greedy? Too land hungry? Much good will it do you.' He was shaking inside but darned if he would show it. Now he needed time to think about his mother and himself.

He left the table, kissing his mother goodbye, William following. He put a few clothes and personal photographs in his case and went to his car. William, leather belt in hand jumped him as he threw his case in the trunk.

He fought but was no match for the older, heavier man and fell to the ground. William continued to vent the frustration of years, kicking and using his belt buckle to cause maximum pain. Before he lost consciousness he thought he heard his mother screaming and Adam laughing.

TWO YEARS LATER.

Nathan was in hospital for many months. He feigned memory loss and inside himself he burned with hate. As his body slowly mended he planned a terrible revenge.

Hospital fees were paid presumably from the farm but he had no visitors. He had a bankbook with five thousand dollars credit. He guessed that his mother was responsible for this. He had read with sadness of her sudden death in the county newspaper and, though no explanation was given he could imagine her state of mind and knew she would have little reason to live, obviously Adam had moved closer to his father.

When he left hospital he went to the coast where he did casual work to regain his strength and refine his plan. He left no forwarding address.

He returned to the farm on the day of the weekly Cattlemans' Association meeting knowing William would be away. Adam was reading on the porch and not a bit fazed to see Nathan. He was rattled though, when Nathan pulled a gun and ordered him inside, taking a length of rope from his waist and leading him to a radiator.

Nathan was silent as he secured Adam who seemed too astounded to protest. He watched as Nathan prowled the room, raising his eyebrows at the heavy draperies, rich furnishings and spectacular native paintings. He stopped before a portrait of William, brooding and powerful hanging above the fireplace. 'Soon' he said 'very soon', and fired three shots at the painted head, leaving a jagged hole and destroying the hated face.

'What the hell are you doing?' the shock had loosened Adam's tongue. 'That portrait cost thousands - are you crazy?'

'No, not crazy. I'm 'phoning the sheriff now to let him know he has a hostage situation. And I want William here.' He spoke briefly into the telephone then hurled it at a remarkably fine American wall clock, smashing the glass.

'Stop it you fool, he'll kill you this time, those are valuable things. No' he screamed as Nathan kicked over a heavy Satsuma urn, then dodged as a chrystal decanter hit the wall beside him, bourbon splashing the carpet. He was in tears now as Nathan silently wreaked havoc in the once lovely room.

'Am I spoiling your toys Adam? You want a museum, not a working ranch you parasite. Did you ever do any real work here?'

'Why do you hate so much? Father gave you a good life.'

'Yeah, always putting me down and what sort of life did he give Mother. Not that you ever cared so long as you could play house.'

There was the sound of cars and sirens through the open window followed by the Sheriff's voice 'Nathan, what the hell are you doing? Come on out of there and bring Adam with you.'

The room was quiet. Outside darkness had fallen. Brilliant lights played over the once sumptuous room, reflecting fire from the chandeliers and showing the stark reality of the ruined pictures.

'Come on Nathan,' boomed William. 'Give up this nonsense, whatever it is you want, you'll get.'

'No, you old fool, you'll never give me what I want' he said quietly. 'He's always hated me' to his brother.

'So what do you want?'

'Too late now. All I ever wanted was to live here and work this farm. Now, well now I just need for him to suffer for a very long time.'

'Haven't you done enough?'

'No.'

Lights probed the windows again and the Sheriff's voice gave it's same message. 'Throw out your weapon and open the door. Come out with you hands above your head.'

Suddenly Nathan raised his gun, firing two shots into an overstuffed armchair. He crossed the room and untied Adam, telling him to stand.

Going to the window he shouted 'I'm coming out now' and threw his gun towards the lights. Gesturing for Adam to follow he went to the massive door, unbolting it. Throwing it wide, he pushed Adam through. Shots rang out and his brother fell.

He stood in the doorway, facing William.

William raised the gun again.

By Roma Butcher.

First Love

And did you dream of soaring through the air
Above the clouds, diving and swooping, eagle proud
Or of brown eyes and honey-scented hair?

Of golden skin, gentle voice and soft breasts
Or loops or barrel rolls among the clouds
Were you dreaming of soaring through the air?

Then did ambition strive to make you best
Or drifting, dreaming did you shout aloud
Of brown eyes and honey-scented hair?

Then did new love give hope and life fresh zest
Or do you search in vain among the crowds
Hopeless, drifting seeking to find her there?

Fond parent now to make the pain far less
Their joys, their skills, achievements make you proud
No thought of brown eyes and honey-scented hair?

Do all dreams fail as days fade in the west?
Do all flames cool, is dreaming not allowed?
No, still you dream of soaring through the air
Seeking brown eyes and honey-scented hair.

By Jack Hopkins

Greeting

'Hi yah! Is that you, Tom?'

With his plastic framed glasses askew, Ray peers through the bottom button-hole on his worn out overcoat. It is held upside down and inside out as for the fifth time he struggles to get himself dressed. He wishes Tom would come by; he likes Tom; he likes the strong sound of his voice. Tom always has time to make a joke with him or tell stories about the war. Ray did not go to the war; he had to look after his sick father. He was the only one left after his two older sisters had both gone back to Ireland.

Tom lives next door. He has been a widower for seven years and lives on his own. He and his wife used to run a small garden centre which they opened after the war. It was more like a village shop really. You could get anything there and to make it even better, Tom would deliver things personally.

When Betty his wife, passed on, Tom gave it up. But, he has remained a good neighbour to Ray.

Ray likes to have Tom around. He tells him stories of his war experiences; Ray likes to listen to his adventures. It fills him with excitement as his imagination takes him to places he would dream of going. Some of Tom's stories seem hard to believe but, who cares – it brightens his day and makes him happy. Unlike the nurse or social care worker.

'WHAT'S HER NAME AGAIN?' he pauses, trying to remember her name.

How often he wonders what she looks like. Is she fattish or skinny? What he does know is that she is very strong as she lifts him off the bed and into his chair in one sweep – an experience that leaves him breathless, with his mind whirling.

His thoughts wander down that trail. He seems to remember she said she came from one of the islands- Columbus Island, one of the little ones. He was never any good at geography and foreign things like that.

'Oh!' he thinks. 'How my memory plays with me these days!'

The loud creak from the door brings him back.

'Hi yah, Tom! Is that you?'

The firm sound of the door shutting tells him it is not Tom.

'It's –WHATS HER NAME AGAIN?'

By Albertha Braithwaite.

Solomon's Secrets

(The following is an excerpt from Chris' novelette, which has the same title)

Chapter One

Sarah lay on top of the bed with her eyes shut, as she checked out that she had done all that she could.

This was certainly a Sunday morning like none in her experience and she still did not understand how things could change so fast. The police appeared attentive but not too concerned when she phoned to report her husband's disappearance. They suggested that there would no doubt be a simple explanation. Their questions had left her confused. Worst of all she had been so embarrassed by her inability to come up with answers regarding Solomon's profession, his history, or even his country of origin. She had tried to explain their whirlwind romance. They had no need for questions.

They had lived for the moment, but now she felt stupid. Next the police had come, and they took some of the contents of his briefcase with them when they left, promising to keep her informed. An appointment would be made for her to visit the station.

At this particular time she preferred to stay at the hotel, in the hope that he would contact her. She wanted a little more time before talking to any friends or family about her new husband. (And his disappearance.)

She remembered him saying, "Sarah." (She loved the way that he said her name, the first 'a' a long drawn out '*aaaah.*') "I am so sorry that I have these business appointments to keep this week. I hate to think of you feeling neglected. Please amuse yourself with the therapies and beauty treatments available here. Go shopping, enjoy yourself. On Friday we'll decide where we go next."

They had hurried to their luxury suite after saying goodbye to their guests at their wedding reception. She remembered how he would throw his head back and laugh with gusto if they witnessed any incident that he thought ridiculous. He laughed very easily. Dark curly hair, thick-lashed dark eyes, and incredibly white teeth. Her one disappointment was that her family and friends had not even met him. Everything had been so rushed.

Chapter Two

Clasped at last in each other's arms he became incredibly seductive. He took his time in peeling off her already skimpy layers of clothing. She had not noticed that he had backed her up to the doorway of their bedroom.

At that very strategic moment the suite bell had rung and a voice announced "Champagne sir, compliments of the house!"

He wanted to ignore it but she'd whispered in his ear, "I'll be in bed, don't be long!" She stepped out of her slip and slid between the sheets.

He never came back. When she got up to investigate, she found the door had been left wide open.

She had not told the police that their marriage had not been consummated. It was too private a matter. It had all seemed like a work of fiction. Such things didn't happen to people like her, 'Sarah Hemmings from Kent.'

She had been visiting London to attend the wedding of an old friend. Solomon had swooped, totally overwhelming her. He talked about love at first sight, and swore undying love. He had persuaded her to extend her stay in London. Gifts and flowers were delivered every day. Exclusive restaurants and hotels were their meeting places every evening. Who could have predicted such a romance? He had laughed at her bewilderment at all the attention she was receiving.

No telephone calls came and Sarah became increasingly tearful. She wandered into the bedroom and lay on top of the duvet. She had meant to bathe and go to bed in the normal way, but fell instead into a restless sleep.

****

She sat up suddenly, hearing voices.

"Very sorry old man, tripped over my own feet. It's so dark in here; I'm feeling a little unsteady."

"Just take your time old fellow, we're in unfamiliar territory don't you know."

For some reason the voices sounded familiar. Sarah switched on the nearest lamp. A portly man with a walrus moustache was rising from the floor still mumbling apologies to his companion standing just behind him. It was the unmistakable figure of Sherlock Holmes. He was looking straight at her. Both figures appeared entirely in monochrome. The colour of Holmes' hatchet-shaped face seemed corpse-like.

He smiled. "Ah, good evening young lady. This might seem terribly confusing, but all will be revealed in a trice. May I sit on the end of your bed?"

Eyes wide open, Sarah found she was nodding consent.

"Thank y-o-u" he said, in a quite exaggerated manner. She closed her eyes, thinking they might vanish or that she would probably wake up. But no. She watched as Holmes removed his cape and deerstalker hat. He then lit his pipe.

Watson began to stammer nervously. "Holmes, I do believe I saw a 'No Smoking' sign as we entered."

"What nonsense, how is a gentleman supposed to work without his pipe? We'll have no further delay."

Sarah, now gradually recovering, became impatient. "How can you be here? You're not even real. You never were. You're just fictional characters. You don't really exist!"

"Ah well, that was very logically thought through m'dear, but it actually doesn't work like that. As characters in a work of fiction we have many followers, devotees who are convinced we are real. It is elementary therefore that it is their belief in us, and the energy it imparts, that allows us a kind of existence. No energy is ever wasted you see. Occasionally we leave Baker Street to assist those experiencing problems such as yourself. Mysteries, murders, and of course that devilish villain Moriarty are our particular speciality."('He's very pompous' she thought.)

"I promise we will leave no stone unturned. I am confident that we will deduce what has happened to your dear Solomon. We shall gain in strength as you come to believe in us."

Holmes leaned forward to pat her hand. She felt nothing.

"Before we proceed with our investigation, would you be so kind as to help us become familiar with this apartment. Gas is our only source of energy back home. These fixtures and fittings look quite peculiar and somewhat threatening. Could you perhaps explain their functions? It will help us focus as we become a little more relaxed about this environment."

"If you insist," she said impatiently. Her watch told her that it was now two-fifty in the morning. She wished she could wake. She imagined Solomon roaring with laughter at this farce. With the remote controls she opened the electric blinds at the wide windows. The illuminated horizon of London appeared below them. Watson leaped back in fear.

"Dear God, are we in the sky?"

"No, just on the twenty-third floor," she replied with a smile.

"Quite fascinating," said Holmes, puffing vigorously at his pipe. The famous detective moved nearer to the window. "London by night *now*, eh? Never been so high in a building." Becoming a little more expansive he went on. "From gas to electricity! Lit like the very stars have fallen from heaven to brighten this sleepless city. Still restless as ever, but with less threatening shadows for footpads and sinful ladies. Nevertheless, crime still thrives. Where there is the temptation of wealth for opportunists, risks will still be taken. The science of forensics may have improved enormously, but society will always require our special skills Watson."

Sarah next proceeded to demonstrate the power shower, the Jacuzzi, the entertainment centre, the air-conditioning system, and finally, the automated bar. She of course found it entirely uninteresting, and marvelled at how engrossed they were. Watson was trembling, whilst Sherlock did his best to appear calm and unimpressed.

At last Holmes said, "Thank you dear lady, now, back to business." He then asked Sarah whether she had searched through Solomon's belongings.

Although she felt foolish she answered very honestly. "Well, no, I left that to the police. You see, I am convinced he'll be back. Searching through his things would seem like an intrusion."

"Well I'm afraid we will have to if we're going to get to the bottom of this mystery," Holmes said firmly. She was asked to spread any papers out so they could examine them. Obediently she began by emptying the pockets of the last jacket he wore. A thick wallet, a mobile phone, and various documents emerged. She found his briefcase and a laptop at the bottom of the wardrobe. She placed everything on the table, then sat in an armchair, watching as they systematically read through every paper. Occasionally they would ask her to turn the pages.

When they had finished, Watson asked her to place all the papers in the pockets of their coats. "Will I be able to do that?" Sarah asked.

"Do you still think that you are dreaming?" the Doctor asked. To her surprise Sarah saw that her visitors had now acquired a sepia hue. This looked a little less spooky but was still quite odd. When the papers slipped into their pockets without effort she felt a definite sense of satisfaction. It was now light outside. The lounge clock read six forty three.

Holmes asked, "Will you be in later this morning and again in the evening?"

"If you need me to be," she replied.

"Doctor Watson and I will return this evening, but expect a lady visitor in the morning. She will not need your help but some peace and quiet, allowing her to work. ... She will probably make use of these machines." Holmes pointed to the laptop and mobile phone.

Holmes and Watson donned their outdoor coats and their hats. Watson, backing away towards the door, doffed his bowler saying, "Goodnight dear lady."

Sherlock walked towards her, bowed, then gently kissed the back of her hand. This time she could feel his warm breath on her skin. Moments after they had left, she could still smell pipe tobacco.

By Chris Lammas

The Traveller's Cemetery.

Alongside the church crooked gravestones are bare.
Old bones long buried; sad souls linger there.
Forgotten and nameless, under rust coloured moss;
Nobody comes now, to remember their loss.
But, in a small corner lay tombstones for kings;
Marble angels and cherubs with golden tipped wings.
Fresh flowers and garlands, bright Rosary beads;
Small posies with ribbons, large, lush, laurel wreaths.
Not for them that grey wasteland, ignored and alone;
When gypsies pass over, they're proudly brought home.
They honour their dead, whether tinker or king.
No man can say they abandon their kin.

Sun shines in their corner, while *niamo* pray near;
`Travel on now, to *charos*, travel on, without fear`

By Patricia Barber

References.

'Niamo' is the Romany word for kinsmen or relatives.
'Charos' is the Romany word for Heaven.
'Gypsy-Jib' A Romany Dictionary by James Hayward.

Kitchen - Fear

The hot, humid evening air hit Stephanie as she left the comfort of her air-conditioned Mercedes. Making her way up the newly gravelled drive to her front door, she felt happy although tired; this might be the last time she trod this familiar path. Ted, her husband, useless sod that he was, would be at his usual place by the word-processor pretending to write a literary masterpiece. "Fat chance" she thought; "not now." But Ted ran towards her as she entered, he looked wide eyed and panic-stricken. "God, surely he doesn't know," she thought.

"Hi darling!" he cried, his forty something face over-animated. "You're home early."

"Mmmmm." She put her bag down and headed for the kitchen. "I need a cup of tea."

"No, don't." He barred her way.

"Don't what?"

"Don't go in there. -- Come into the lounge -- have a gin and tonic." She allowed herself to be pulled past the closed kitchen door.

"What on earth is going on? You're not cooking are you? Forty is too young to die."

"No, no, it's not that." His hands shook as he poured the drinks. "*He's* in there."

"Who's in there?" She sipped her drink. -- He gulped his.

"*Him*. You know, my Tutor from college; the writer. The bloke you fancy, John Goodfellow."

She nearly choked. "I most certainly do not." Then she gulped. "Anyway, what's he doing in my kitchen?" She turned and headed in that direction.

"Oh, for God's sake no!" Ted grabbed her arm. "You don't understand, he's reading my manuscript -- I've finished it." He puffed himself up.

She looked incredulous. "I don't believe it. After seven years you've actually finished something, the literary version of the unfinished symphony?" she mocked. "What did you do, spend a week to come up with 'The End'?" She used her hand to hyphenate the phrase.

Ted felt mixed emotions; he looked at his beautiful wife, in full bloom at forty, a successful company lawyer. The woman he loved, the woman who had kept him, made him better after the hell he had translated into his masterpiece; why did she mock him?

"Don't you realise darling, it's the biggest day of my life. He's got friends, here and abroad who will publish it if he likes it. He wanted to be alone to read it, but I won't let it out of the house, so he's in there with the manuscript and the discs on the other processor; he's got everything he needs." Once started Ted couldn't stop. "Don't you see, if he likes it I'm in. -- We're in. I'll be an equal, whole again."

"You poor bloody dreamer" Stephanie thought. She spoke. "So this bloke is in my kitchen, drinking my tea, reading your story which you never let *me* read. Knowing you writer types he's probably polished off my Hobnobs too."

"You know I didn't want you to read it until I'd finished. I had to live through those years of hell; only *I* could write it. I experienced it Steph, the depths to which mankind can stoop. Every time I wrote something it was like reopening a wound; blood pouring onto the paper, not ink. I had to live it Steph."

She baulked. The fire was back in Ted's eyes. This was the man she fell in love with. She *had* read it of course. She knew computers inside out as she knew Ted, there was no hiding it from her. And true, it *was* brilliant; -- a masterpiece. But life goes on. The drinks were finished.

"I don't have time for this Ted. You know I've got a business trip to Geneva tomorrow." It wasn't Geneva, and it certainly wasn't business; not in Atlanta, US of A.

"Look Steph, he's been in there a couple of hours now, he must soon have the gist of it. Let him finish. -- It's vital to me. -- To us. I daren't go in there, not yet."

"Well I dare. I've got a lot to do." She hadn't actually; it was all done, Cash from the re-mortgage, cash from the Company, everything from their joint account, airline tickets in her bag.

"Please darling, just for me -- Let him finish."

"I think we've done enough for you in this marriage, don't you?" She pulled away and marched to the kitchen door. Ted stood mortified as she breezed in. "God, I hope she doesn't ruin it." There were no words for what seemed a long time. Gingerly he followed.

"Where is he then?" She gestured to the empty room.

"Oh my God!" John wasn't there, and neither was the manuscript, neither were the discs. Stephanie knew they would all be safely aboard the Atlanta flight, as he spoke. She wondered if it was a good time to tell Ted that he was going back to that Hell he'd lived through. He shouldn't have tried to inflict it on her.

By Simon Butcher

Villanelle Unchained!

Do not speak to me like that.
I know my speech is now slow
But my brain's still sharp as a tack.

I fought in the war and in fact
Was one of the few that so much was owed to, so
Do not speak to me like that.

There's no need to tell me things twice
I hear quite clear but you mumble
My memory holds facts like a vice.

Give me respect. Treat me as a man.
Life in here would make a saint grumble
There's no need to shout 'cause I need a bedpan.

I don't moan though I'm always in pain
I just need help if I stumble.
I've still got a perfectly good brain.

What, what, what's that you said?
No it wasn't me that wet my bed.
Don't speak to me like that.
My brain's still sharp as a tack.

By Jack Hopkins

I Was Known As A Dreamer.

Born into a large family, I was the second eldest of four and given the responsibility of going into town for my mother, who was very near to the birth of her fifth baby. It was 1948 when people were emerging from the wear and tear of the war, into feelings of hopefulness. The village where I lived, on the outskirts of town, was like a close knit family, each, although argumentative at times, like neighbours often are, made a point of looking out for one another.

Children were allowed to remain children, and if one misbehaved, it was acceptable to receive a slap from your elders. One of the warnings received from my parents was, 'don't talk to strangers'. Had I only listened to my mother that particular day; but then I was known as a dreamer, my mind always somewhere else.

'Put your Sunday best on Aileen, I need you to do some shopping for me', said my mother, just as I was getting stuck into my favourite comic. As a nine year old I thought I knew everything, but I loved going into town and within ten minutes I was ready. I was told what to get and was given a half crown. But, even before I reached the end of the narrow lane I heard my mother shout after me.

'Don't forget Aileen, go into O'Malley's first and order the oats, then go to Gormand's yard and order the coal. Tell him to deliver not later than tomorrow afternoon, and to collect the oats on the way; he knows the routine by now. And don't lose the half crown like you did before!'

'I'll hold on to it Mamma, I promise'

'Don't linger, I want you home by teatime'.

I nodded my head waving goodbye, humming to myself as I left the lane, waving to old Peter who was sitting on the long stone bench outside the front window of his cottage that was situated facing the main road into town. I knew if I did a quick run I would get into the town centre in under half an hour; but it was a beautiful day, blue skies as far as the eyes could see. My hand dug into the pocket of my pale pink dress feeling the roundness of the half crown, and I knew there was a penny change to buy my favourite Dab-Dab lolly. The road narrowed and widened as I went along and the only traffic that passed me were two horses, their riders calling me by name as they went on their way to the stables, where my father worked as a stable hand.

When I entered O'Malley's shop, it was almost empty of customers, so he was able to give me his full attention, even allowing me to dip into the long stemmed glass jar and take out two Dab-Dabs instead of the usual one, after I told him the tomatoes in our greenhouse would be ready for collecting by the weekend. As I came out of the shop, I collided with two of the tallest strangers I had ever seen. I apologised in my usual shy manner, dropping one of my Dab-Dabs. But before I could bend down to pick it up, it was picked by the nearest stranger. This was a stout, blonde haired, red cheeked woman, who smiled at me with a mouthful of large square, and even teeth; I thought for a minute I was looking into the mouth of a horse. She called me Pauline, in a long drawn out American accent, holding my Dab-Dab, then dusting it with the tips of her red painted nails.

'Your lolly, Pauline' she said, putting it into my hand, and then patting my shoulder. I thanked her shyly trying to move away, but they were still blocking my path; the man behind much taller than the woman, casting a shadow over me. They were so large and well fed. I felt so small and not used to tackling such strange people; I wondered what to do next. I asked them if I could pass, looking more up their noses than their faces, but they just stared down at me, smiling broadly. Seconds went by, then suddenly they moved aside and

I was sure it was the alarm on my face that did it. I walked quickly away towards Gorman's yard, some distance along the same side of the road. I felt safe in the yard, taking my time in ordering the coal and mentioning the oats. When I came out there was no sign of the Americans, so I soon forgot their existence, making my way until I turned into O'Connor Street. Half way up, I bumped into my school chums and stood chatting about this and that. We were two weeks into summer holidays, which meant freedom from the strictness of the nuns in the convent school we attended. Looking at the forming clouds in the sky, I though about what my mother had said about hurrying home, so with a wave I moved on. The rain came down suddenly I had to run for shelter into the nearest doorway of the three storey Victorian house that had a pillared glass archway fringing some feet out to the edge of the pathway.

A lot of such houses, some dating back more than two hundred years, adorned both sides of the street; with the odd shop or church breaking up their neatness.

While I was standing there, a large black car, with shiny chrome handles, pulled up and once I recognised the tall strangers, The man behind the wheel was beckoning me to come forward; his snow white hair cut short, showing very large ears. Seeing the danger, and my parents warning, I looked around to try to make a dash for it, but the woman got out of the car and was blocking my way. She touched my face, calling me Pauline. I backed away until my back was pushing against the door. She reached out to take my hand, but I quickly turned around and tried to ring the doorbell. In doing so my hand was forced away from the bell and somehow through a mist of terror I found my voice and clear as I could I said,

'Go away, I'm not Pauline, my name is Aileen'.

I could see the rain was still pelting down, and like me everyone had run for shelter. I felt sick to my stomach and had no experience whatsoever of how to handle such a tricky situation. As much as I tried my voice failed to make any more noise.

'We will take you home, Pauline. Mummy will get very cross if you disobey us. Your beautiful dress and sandals are getting ruined. This must not happen, darling'

I knew I was no match for them. Again I turned around to try to ring the doorbell, even tried to bang on the door, but my hand was held and pushed down by my side. To me at that moment time stood still. I was moving along, her hand firmly holding mine. Desperately, I looked round to spot a familiar face as I was lifted into the back seat of the car, the stout woman getting in beside me. She was wearing strong perfume, making me feel quite queasy. I tried to make an effort to move out of her way, my voice at last belting out,

'Let me go, I want my Ma. Take your hands off me!'

But try as I did, my words were drowned out by the clap of thunder, and the closeness of her body as she cradled me in her arms, muttering, 'Pauline. My Pauline', over and over again.

'We are taking you home, darling', they both said together, in their long drawn out American accent. The car was moving with speed along the top of O'Connor Street until it crossed into Crosby Road, where it had to slow down. It was then I got a glimpse of a few faces I knew as they crossed the road, but before I could shout, a hand was put over my mouth. Then the car moved away and, as she released her hand from my mouth, I let out an almighty scream; I paid dearly for it. She shook me roughly, pushing me against the hard seat, banging my head, her grip tighter this time. The car suddenly jerked to a halt, letting a horse drawn carriage pass, releasing her grip for a few seconds; giving me the opportunity to make a bolt for the door. Thomas, the delivery boy, was passing on his bike. I banged on the door window as he passed, seeing his eyes widen in surprise, taking in my frightened face. But again, before I could get the door open, the woman pulled me back and slapped me hard on the side of my face; I slumped to the floor in tears.

'Sit back and behave yourself, Pauline, or, I will put you in the boot of the car like I did before'. That added to my fears, which were already mounting rapidly. But her voice grew soft, pulling me up and seating me next to her. 'You've lost your ribbon, Pauline. Your plait has come undone. Let Mummy brush your hair out'.

She started on my plait, which ran the full length of my back. Unable to do very much, my stomach knotted into sheer panic, and sick with fear, I let her plait my hair, bringing it over my shoulders to the front.

'I want to go home', I begged more than once. 'Please let me out. My name is Aileen, not Pauline'.

But for all the notice that they took of my pleading, I might just as well have kept quiet. The car took up speed along the main road going towards my home, but it was also the way to Dublin and other cities. I sat in frozen stillness while she rooted in her large bag bringing out a hairbrush. We were near the opening of the lane to my home, and I could see old Peter's cottage, but, there was no sign of him as we passed. With gripping fear I found my voice again,

'Please let me go. I won't tell anybody. Me Ma will have my tea ready. You can come if you like, she likes Americans'.

I could see the glittering blue eyes of the man in the mirror in front. He was smiling at me, adding to my fears.

'We won't harm you Pauline. We are taking you home to America. They said you were dead, but they were wrong. We found you here in Ireland, and no one is going to take you away from us again', he remarked , his drawn out voice bouncing around the interior of the car, sending shivers all over my body. The woman was still brushing my hair, and in a dreamlike state I let her. But my father's voice penetrated my shocked brain.

'Back up for yourself, Aileen' he had said, when not so long ago a bully in the school kept tormenting me in the playground, jeered on by her chums. I had bruises to show many a time, after she elbowed me to the ground as I passed.

I heeded my father's advice and the opportunity came when we met each other in the toilets. I took my time, and as she went into one of the cubicles, I followed her with pent up anger, sticking her head down the toilet as I flushed it, and as she emerged spluttering for air, holding her head down and flushing it again. That did the trick. She left me alone after that and went after some other unfortunate victim.

The woman was still brushing my hair, tilting my chin so she could brush my fringe. I could see the opening to the lane, to the stables, where my father worked, some way ahead, and I had to do something fast. My hair was now fluffy and bouncy, and both the strangers appeared relaxed and smiling. Now I know for a fact that if you want an adult to move fast, and as far away from you as possible, you only have to utter these few words, and shake your head vigorously. I could see the opening to the lane getting nearer; my father's voice gave me the courage, moving a few inches away I said, loud and clear.

'I've got fleas and nits, lots of them. I don't want them; I'm giving them to you'.

I put my hands behind my neck bringing my hair forward then shook my head until my hair spread everywhere. The woman's shocked eyes stared at me, moving right back in her seat. Then I stood up as far as I could, wrapping my hands around the driver's face, then digging my fingers into his eyes. He let out a loud cry in pain. The woman tried to grab me, but I became as slippery as an eel. The car zigzagged along the road until it jerked to a stop a few feet before the entrance to the lane. I knew I had hurt the American, I could feel the softness of his eyeball as I stuck my finger in. With speed I tugged at the handle of the car door until it opened, giving me the chance to jump out, but in doing so I fell into a side ditch that was swollen by the rain. Scrambling out and feeling the thorny brambles tear at my hands and face, I wasted no time racing the few feet, rounding into the lane and running as fast as I could. I could see the stables, but they were a long way up.

Not knowing if I could make it or not, I kept running, my eyes taking in the riders dismounting and handing the reins over to the stable hands. My father was there somewhere I kept thinking as I stumbled a few times, feeling the small sharp stones cutting my knees. Within a minute I heard the roar of the engine, and without looking back I knew they had turned into the lane. It was only a matter of seconds before they would draw level with me, or run me down. But their car had stopped and seconds later I could hear their heavy footsteps not far behind. I had to look behind and in doing so I stumbled into the muddy side ditch, the stump of thin wood protruding from the ground going straight through my knickers. I screamed in agony, grabbing at the stems of tall grass until I made it out of the ditch, racing only yards ahead of them. Then I spotted my father, adjusting the saddle on a horse, then bending down, his hands fastening the straps under the horse's belly.

'Da' I shouted as loud as I could, 'Da, look around! It's me. Help me'.

The footsteps faded away from behind me, and the only sound was my feet pounding on the sharp pebbles, my breath coming gasps. I screamed out once more with every breath in my body.

'Dada, help me'.

He must have heard me for he straightened up, turning around, his hand going to his eyes to shield them from the sun. Then he was running towards me, faster than a galloping horse. He was also shouting to whoever was there in the enclosure. My father reached me first, scooping me into his arms and holding me tight. His first words were,

'God Almighty! What have they done to my little girl; she's covered in blood. Get the bastards', he shouted to the riders who had circled around us.

He was kissing my face, the tears streaming down his cheeks. I felt safe; I didn't need to shout anymore. My father's eyes were all over me,

'Did they do this to you, dearest', he asked, choking back the sobs. I nodded my head before saying,

'I jumped out of their car. Don't let them near me Da, I'm afraid of them. They want to take me back to America. Don't let them, Da'. I could feel myself getting very wet. Something was running down my legs.

'Da, I'm sorry, I've peed myself. I need to go to the toilet'.

When I tried to look down at my feet, my father blocked my view with his hand.

'Don't look down dearest, just a few drops of blood, that's all. Soon have you cleaned up. You're safe now, I won't leave you'.

A blanket was thrown round my father covering both of us completely, and a female voice I recognised as Polly, the housekeeper, was wiping my face with a flannel; kissing me and telling me I was safe. When we turned towards the stables, I managed to look down the lane. A group of riders with whips raised high were lashing out at the two Americans. I could hear their screams above the shouts of the angry riders. The entrance to the lane was blocked by two police cars, the policemen running towards the crowd, and I thought thankfully, Thomas had spotted me and reported it to the police. My name was called a few times, and people were touching my cheeks, but I felt so cold and sleepy, even though the blanket was still wrapped around us. My father's voice penetrated the numbness of my brain a few times and I managed to give him a weak smile. I could see the big house ahead and an ambulance coming towards us. Then two men were rushing down the narrow path with a trolley. My father placed me on the trolley and I was piled high with blankets. I felt so sleepy and cold, even when I was briefly examined in the ambulance, I didn't move. My father's eyes never left my face. I felt safe; that was all that mattered to me at that moment.

I tried to cry when the ambulance started up, the noise from the siren making me shudder, but no sound came, so I gave up. When I looked at the dark stains on my father's riding breeches, I knew it was blood; I didn't pee myself. My father kept his eyes on my face, his hand reaching over and resting on my shoulder. Too exhausted now I closed my eyes, and then heard the alarm in my father's voice. He shook me gently, so did the ambulance man, urging me to try to stay awake a little longer. I tried, but failed, my brain blocking out everything, even my father's voice, trailing off like an echo. The last thing I remembered was something closing over my face, the rush of air into my mouth and nose.

When I woke up, I was in a single room, in a bed with cot sides up. My granny was sitting near on a chair that seemed too small for her heavy frame. She was watching me closely and smiling. My granddad came in then, his tall, lanky frame bending over to kiss me on the cheek.

'Where's me Ma and Da?' I asked, looking around. My granddad answered in a soft voice.

'Your Ma came yesterday, but you were asleep. You have a new little baby sister. Your Ma will visit as soon as she is allowed, and your Pa will be here shortly. Are you well enough to answer a few questions?' I nodded my head, watching him turn to say something to my granny. She left the room.

'Granny is getting you a glass of milk. Now there is no need to be afraid, I will be with you. There will be a couple of policemen asking you about your kidnappers. Just tell them as it happened. Leave nothing out. Start from the time you first set eyes on them. Can you do that Aileen?' I nodded my head again.

'Good girl. You will be coming home with us for the time being. Your Ma and Pa will visit you there'.

'Why am I not going home?' I asked. My granddad replied, gently taking my hand.

'We are the nearest to the hospital, and you will have to come here daily for treatment. But there is no need for you to feel afraid of the kidnappers. They are in jail. Remember you asked about the King and Queen of England and famous places in London?'

'Yes, and you said you would tell me when you have got the time', I answered, sitting up, my head against the iron head rest. My granddad reached for the pillow that was at the end of the bed, tucking it down my back, before he said,

'I managed to get you a book about England. It's got a lot of pictures of places in London'. He took the book out of his coat pocket, opening the front page showing Buckingham Palace. My eyes lit up with delight.

'I'll take care of it. Do you want it back granddad?'

'No, it's a present from your gran and myself. I've ordered some more books. It may take time for them to arrive; you need to share them with Noreen'.

My father came an hour later and stayed as long as he could, and for the next few days policemen and plain clothes officers asked me question after question, their notebooks and pencils continually in motion, until they were satisfied. Then they left, and so did I, into the care of my grandparents who lived in the centre of the town. I stayed with them for a week, then I went home, guarded all the way by my granddad and Uncle Patrick. I had done that journey many times on my own, so when I asked the reason I was told I was not well enough to travel on my own. I was met with a wall of silence about the kidnappers for the next few weeks. The Americans were mentioned, but never in front of me. I knew they were in jail, and a team of American solicitors were representing them. Also, I heard my mother mention to Auntie Flora about a psychiatrist being present, and the death of their six year old child, but they moved away out of earshot before I could hear anymore. But whatever it was, I was guarded, and moved near my parents bedroom. Our four bedroom, two hundred year old cottage was really two semis knocked into one and as we got older we were moved to the bedrooms farthest away. As the second eldest, I shared a room with my elder sister, Noreen. Now I shared a room with my new born sister, Tessa. I questioned it a few times, but gave up when I was told they would explain later. Nearly a month had passed when an opportunity came to talk to my father. when I spotted him sitting on a low rough stone wall in front of our cottage. I joined him, climbing onto the wall, shuffling myself nearer to him. He was his usual quiet self, engrossed in rolling his own cigarettes, licking the edge of the paper, then pressing it with his fingers.

'Can I go up the lane Da? There is a game of rounders on and as I am the captain they need me there. Audie came to see me yesterday and they miss me'.

I looked up the lane as far as my eyes could see and pictured some of my chums playing in the square, a short distance from the grocery shop, and the graveyard at the front of the church. Most of the forty or so houses were under twenty years old, and the old blacksmith and adjoining cottage were now converted into a doctor's surgery. But my father was shaking his head,

'Just another day, Aileen, then you can go where you like'.

'Why, Da? I need to know. Did I do something wrong? I'm nine years old; I share a room with my baby sister. Nobody will tell me about the Americans. I heard someone say they were out of jail'. My father's eyes took in both sides of the lane before he answered.

'You did nothing wrong, dearest, if anything, you were very brave. I will tell you about the kidnappers. It's a very tragic story'. He paused putting the unlit cigarette into his mouth, then taking it out again and putting it into his top pocket.

'A couple of months ago, they had a very healthy six year old daughter named Pauline. Their only daughter, I might add. They were putting the finishing touches to her coming seventh birthday, which was a few days away. She complained of a headache, and on her birthday she died of meningitis. As a special treat they were taking her on a tour of Ireland, which they had visited some years ago. When they bumped into you outside O'Malley's store, in their eyes they were looking at their daughter'.

'I'm not their daughter, Da. Surely they must have noticed that?'

'No Aileen dearest. I figured in their traumatized state of mind, they were suffering from such a deep, unexpected loss, and to make matters worse, seeing you looking so uncannily like their daughter made them snap mentally'. I watched my father scan both sides of the lane before continuing.

'I saw a photo of their daughter. It was like looking at you, even to the one plait down your back. They are insane with grief, their mind refusing to believe she died. Believe me, dearest, they adored her. We must find it in our hearts to forgive them'.

'Where are they now, Da?'

'They are in the asylum, and leaving for America this afternoon with a team of doctors; that's if they catch the woman who gave them the slip this morning as they were handing them over to the escorts'.

'Is that why you are here, and Uncle Patrick is in the back garden walking around the orchard?'

'Yes, somehow she knows where you live and may very well make her way here. We need to be alert until they catch her'. My father reached to the side of him where a pile of newspapers lay, unwrapping them until he pulled out some comics and a few old books, handing them to me, he said,

'Hold on for Noreen, share when she comes back from her Granny'.

The pile of comics and books remained on my lap, my attention drawn to the police car coming up the lane, only stopping when it drew level with the front of our cottage. My father got off the wall, telling me to go inside, greeting the policeman with a nod as he got out of the car, and they both walked across the lane into the nearest open gate; disappearing into the field behind the tall bushes, deep in conversation. Within seconds my mother came down the pathway. I told her where my father was. She passed me telling me over her shoulder, to go inside and stay with Auntie Flora, who was baking cakes in the kitchen. When I hesitated she gave me one of her "do as you are told" looks, fluffing up her red hair and wiping her hands on her pinny. I jumped off the wall, but before I reached the front door I took one look around to see my mother disappearing into the field; but I also saw the American woman crouching down inside the wall. Backing away with shock, the woman no more than a breath away, I screamed so loud that within seconds Uncle Patrick was in front of the cottage, restraining the woman who was calling out,

'Pauline, come to Mummy. You are coming back to America with us'.

My Auntie Flora shot to my side pushing me indoors, bolting the door and guiding me into the open plan kitchen and sitting room; leaving me for a few seconds while she bolted the back door and windows. She then told me to stay near my three year old brother who was sleeping in the cot, near the fireplace at the far end of the sitting room. I started to sob, the shock of seeing the woman so near sending fear through every nerve in my body. But, my auntie, being a no nonsense person, told me to shut up, so I suppressed the sobs as best I could, sitting in the rocking chair, my hand over my mouth, and my uncontrollable shaking rocking the chair into motion. My auntie came to my side telling me not to worry, holding my hands, until the knocking on the door and my parents' voices telling her to open it. I moved to the front window just in time to see the ambulance drive away, followed by the police car

My parents were quickly by my side allowing me to cry, while each in turn hugged me, reassuring me the woman was on her way to the airport; encouraged by her husband who had come to terms with the death of his daughter. But the shaking took longer to subside, even my favourite comics and a Dab-Dab did little to disperse the fear. It took days to return to near normality, and a lot of reassuring by my parents that the Americans were in a secure place in America, and they would receive the best of care to make them better, and I would never see them again. But some children are very resilient and, I'm glad to say I was one of them.

Within weeks I was back to my happy self with other things on my mind, and back as captain of the rounders team in the square.

Did I ever get myself into a dangerous, tricky situation again?

Well, yes. But there's reality and dreams. I tend to do the latter; I was known as a dreamer.

By Mary Ann Naicker

The Age Of Innocence

Charles Frost switched off the TV at the end of the news. There seemed nothing worth watching these days. Maybe he'd glance again at the newspaper but it did not keep his attention. It was that last item in the news that was stirring old memories. It had been about a fire near The Royal Forest Hotel in Epping Forest. Epping Forest, he mused. It must be over fifty years ago and yet so easy to remember:

They had all arranged to meet on the bank holiday at ten o'clock at North Chingford Station. There must have been about twenty of them. Charlie could not remember who suggested it but most of those at the youth club the previous Thursday evening seemed to think it was a good idea.

He could not remember all the names, maybe most of them. They were all sixteen or seventeen year old. The club had been the result of the dancing classes held at the boys' grammar school. The girls arrived from the Girls County High school in the neat green blazers and skirts and sat along one side of the hall while Charlie and his class, in grey trousers with navy blazers sat opposite. One lesson per week for a whole term had encouraged his class to think that pressing their chests against soft bosoms was more stimulating than any other lessons on the time-table.

Kenny, who seemed to have an excessive dose of hormones, wanted the liaisons to continue. John's father, who was the Congregational Minister at the church near the top of Walthamstow High Street, agreed that a club could meet in the church hall every Thursday evening. It was that club that crossed over the road outside the station and straggled over Chingford Plain towards The Royal Forest Hotel.

David was explaining to Jean why the plain had regular ridges all along its length and she, politely appearing interested, quietly listened. They passed the hotel, heading for Connaught Waters, sometimes singing or laughing or chatting. The lake was surrounded by mud so they wandered between huge oaks and hornbeams. Never, to Charlie had the world seemed so at peace. The sun filtered dancing beams on to Heather's hair. "She is so beautiful" thought Charlie. He had never dared to speak to her.

Derek, Charlie's best friend, was talking to Jean and Brenda. Jean wore glasses, which made her appear serious but Brenda was lively and always willing to burst in to peals of laughter. Just ahead were June and Sylvia. June was wearing too tight short shorts and a buttoned stressed white blouse. Kenny and Peter were walking just behind the two girls singing: "June is bustin' out all over."

They emerged from the forest to a large grassy area where there were wooden seats and, across a small road, a large Pub called the Bald Faced Stag.

Someone produced an old tennis ball and with a bit of wood for a bat, they played rounders. Muriel, whose bust had pressed itself to Charlie's chest in many a dance lesson, swished at the ball, missed and when she ran, screeched and wobbled, losing all her charm. Kenny, of the excessive hormones, had told Charlie, in confidence of course, that he had taken her to the cinema last Saturday and afterward in some discreet corner had explored her anatomy.

"She just stood there," he said "Just stood there like the bleedin' statue of liberties." He seemed quite upset as though he would have preferred some resistance. Charlie had been interested; he had never met a girl so generous with her mysteries.

Jean, glasses gleaming in the sun, whacked the ball and ran with effortless elegance. She was, Brenda explained, captain of the school tennis team.

Derek had negotiated, through the door of the Bald Faced Stag and several jugs of still lime squash and paper cups brought the sports to an end. Most of the girls had rolls or sandwiches, Charlie and all of the boys were happy to cadge off the girls.

And then, August bank holiday reverted to type. Black skies, strong winds, cats and dogs! They were saturated by the time they again reached the railway station. But, it seemed, nobody wanted the day to end. David said it was certain that they could open the church hall that evening and finally all agreed to go home, get dried and ready for a party evening.

The rain had relented when Charlie arrived at the church hall. Word of mouth had increased the numbers a little. Best of all for Charlie, Sylvia Elst was there. She was a recent arrival from Sweden, a magical blonde with the added ingredient of foreign allure. There were only about 6 records to pick from and Charlie had made his move when "The Sleepy Lagoon" hit the turntable for the second time. They waltzed. She was like a feather in his arms. They said nothing.

Unfortunately, with such limited records, the Tango, Jealousy, came around with too soon frequency.

Charlie always danced with Jean, of the glasses, for the Tango. Neither could dance it but Charlie felt at ease with Jean, they would joke, she would laugh with him and their parody of the tango dance seemed to give them pleasure. Kenny fancied himself as an Al Jolson imitator and always sang along loudly to "Rosie you are my po-sy."

Charlie was not sure if this was a quick, slow fox trot or a slow, quick –step and so he shuffled around with Jean. She was singing softly, "You are my heart's bouquet." She had a sweet, gentle voice.

At ten o'clock sharp, the evening finished. Some turned left outside the hall to pick up a bus in Hoe Street while Charlie and a few others walked together down the High Street. Kenny, Heather, Sylvia and others, turned off at the Palmerston Road. Charlie found himself walking alone with Jean. More surprising still, they were walking hand in hand. It felt so good, so peaceful.

At the bottom of the High Street was Lidstones, a large department store, owned by Jean's father. The family lived in a large apartment above the store.

They stopped in the doorway and Charlie leant forward to kiss her good-night. Her glasses hit the side of his eyes. Jean took her glasses off and they tried again. Her lips were cool, her hair smelled of fresh soap.

As Charlie continued his walk home it rained again. Water seeped in to his right shoe and his toes squelched in his soggy sock. What a perfect day, he thought.

Charles Frost, singing gently to himself, "Rosie you are my po-sy," got up from his chair as he heard his wife returning from her visit to their latest grandchild. I'll put the kettle on, he thought; Jean will want a nice cup of tea.

By Jack Hopkins

The Manipulator

She had dressed carefully for this part. She had always been good at drama in school. She chose him carefully, convincing him of her naivety. She had taken this route regularly, playing the part of a kind, and slightly stupid girl, who was anxious about her parents wearing themselves down while they tried to look after her Nan. She told him that it was her duty to become the old lady's carer.

"My Mum and Dad are looking so tired; they've had no rest for the past five years since Granddad died."

That evening it had begun to rain, and the dusty old cobbles were shining beneath the dim streetlights. The sombre East End houses on either side were mainly unlit.

"It's dodgy walking round here at night, it's so dark." He had persuaded her to let him walk with her part of the way. He had been there every evening this week to walk with her. With deliberate innocence the girl had let him know that the old lady was very frail, staying in bed most of the time, prone to leaving the door unlocked. She remarked how worrying it was that her Nan left money and jewellery laying around the house, refusing to let the family place it in a bank.

"She's so stubborn!" said the girl. "What would you do?"

He shrugged. "I don't know."

As they neared the street corner the young girl thanked him. "I'm going to pop into Auntie's; I've got a cake for her that Mum made. Goodnight. --- I may see you tomorrow."

She walked on, certain that he would make his way to Nan's house. The old lady was such an easy target, almost a gift. She turned once he was out of sight, and began the final part of the walk. She had been careful to spoil her Grandmother just enough to guarantee that the old dear would change her will so that she would inherit everything. She had convinced the old lady that her parents had turned their backs. Long used to using the threat of changing her will to manipulate her family, Grandma had fallen for it.

The girl watched as his long shadow disappeared through the doorway. After a while she pushed the door open; she saw him busily searching the drawers for anything of value. She saw her Grandmother lying very still on the bed; she was definitely dead. He had used the red cushion from the armchair to suffocate her.

"Did you find what you were looking for?" she asked calmly.

He spun round and began to approach her. She fired Granddad's pistol squarely into his chest. He slumped forward into a heap; a gold locket he was holding slipping gently out of his hand onto the floor. The girl felt strangely calm. It had all happened according to plan, and just as she had imagined. She couldn't have acted the caring role for much longer.

"I'll be off" she thought. "Just as soon as the hoo-ha settles down and the will has been processed."

She was now ready to play out the next scene. Looking in the mirror she felt the tears fall down her cheeks, just as she has rehearsed. Tying the hood of her red cape around her pretty young face, she began screaming for help.

By Chris Lammas

Mother Love

Tight clasp of her hand around my finger
From the moment of her birth she was gone
No backward glance or time to linger

Making my gladdened heart take wing
Her eyes already ahead, love that shone
Tight clasp of her hand around my finger

So much happiness her years did bring
Moulding herself to my arms until grown
No backward glance or time to linger

Urgencies of her world too rushed to ring
Surely a mother can have one to belong
Tight clasp of her hand around my finger

Her childhood as magical as Spring
Stay with me until I grow stronger
No backward glance or time to linger

Always I will hear her call and nothing
Will stop my circling arms holding you longer
Tight clasp of her hand around my finger
No backward glance or time to linger

By Pamela Harris

The Train Of Lost Souls

She had no idea what time it was. Just that it was very late. The Tube Train rattled on through the darkness with the familiar clickety-clack and the occasional squeal from the brakes. She was very tired. ------ Daydreaming part of the time, and otherwise trying to amuse herself reading the advertisements.

The pipes and cables that lined the tunnel wall made an ever-changing pattern through the grimy windows. It was very hypnotic, and coupled with the rocking motion of the carriage, it started to send her to sleep. She shook her head and looked around. There were the usual late night travellers. Well dressed couples obviously returning from the Theatre or Cinema, one or two families with small children who had probably been on a trip to see the museums or art galleries, and the odd City type like herself who had been working late. There were also a few weirdos in strange costumes, she thought they might have been to a fancy-dress party.

She started to doze again. She thought dreamily that it would be nice to be tucked up in bed, her husband's warm body pressed against hers in sleep, his arm protectively around her waist. It amused her to think that no matter what position they were in when they went to sleep; they always ended up like spoons. Very conducive to peaceful dreams though.

Janet (That was her name) woke with a start. "How much longer to Walthamstow Central?" she thought. She knew there was a very long stretch between Finsbury Park and Seven Sisters, perhaps that was where they were. She started to scan the advertisements again, and that was when the nightmare began. She closed her eyes and then opened them again. No, it was still the same. ----- Pears Soap? What was an advert for Pears Soap doing in a modern Tube Train? There were other outdated adverts too, Dr Collis-Browne's Remedy, Reckitt's Blue, Edwards Soups, and Carter's Little Liver Pills.

She looked around wildly, to see if any of the other passengers had noticed. The light was much dimmer than it had been before, and she saw with horror that where there had previously been bright electric lights there were now flickering oil-lamps. The passengers looked different too. The women all wore ankle length dresses and bonnets, and the men wore Edwardian clothes, some with tall hats. Most of the men sported long side-whiskers and moustaches.

The weirdos were still there; there was a Vicar, a Tart, and a Clown. On closer inspection, she saw that in fact, they were not wearing fancy dress. The Vicar was clearly a man of the cloth, and the Tart was a blowsy middle-aged woman wearing a split skirt and fishnet stockings who looked as if she had just walked in off the street. "Beam me up Scotty," moaned Janet.

In her distress she let out a strangled sob, and the Tart looked towards her. "Are you alright Dearie?" she said, as she tottered across on her ridiculous high heels.

"I just want to go home," whimpered Janet, "I don't know what's going on."

The Tart clucked sympathetically. "Don't you worry sweetheart, I'll look after you. ---- See, what's happened dear, now brace yourself, ---- you've passed over."

Instantaneously, vividly, a scenario imprinted itself on Janet's consciousness. King's Cross Tube Station, rush hour, impossible crowd on the platform, train approaching, a surge forward, a screaming figure falls in the path of the train. She knew with grim certainty that the figure was her. She stood up and looked up and down the length of the carriage. "My poor Sam," she murmured.

 "Yes, quite a shock," said the Tart. --------- "He's on his way to identify the body now. ----- What's left of it."

Janet looked tearfully at her self-appointed mentor. "Why have we gone back to Edwardian times?"

"Well, you see, this train, The Train of Lost Souls it's called, goes on a very wide circuit, and it goes through a number of time zones."

"Oh," said Janet. She paused, trying to take in the enormity of her situation. She sat down. The Tart, attentive as ever, sat next to her, primly pulling down her skirt as Janet turned to her. "How long will it be before we get to Heaven?" she asked.

"Oh dear," said the Tart, "You're not very bright, are you dear? Look!" And she pointed toward the front of the carriage.

Even in the dim light, it was possible to see the coach in front and just about into the one in front of that. If you watched, you could see the train snaking around the bends in the tunnel. Janet could also see the gradient. ---- The coach they were in was higher than the one in front, and it was clear that the tunnel was heading unmistakably and inexorably downwards.

She looked at the Tart resignedly and said, "Oh, what the Hell!"

By Bill Davies

All About Me.

Now I'm a bit fed up with me
For nothing's going right.
I've a really sorely knee
And I look a sorry sight.

Last week I caught a cold
From looking in the freezer.
I'd forgotten where I hold
My stock of Bacardi Breezer.

When I found them I had three
Then walked right through a window
Just as far as the old apple tree
And the branch that hangs so low.

Dazed, I thought I'd hibernate
Keep quiet, eat well and adjust.
I did keep quiet but ate and ate
And had bellyache fit to bust.

Whatever next I thought
Can go so wrong with me.
Then I got particularly fraught
When I made a cup of tea.

The kettle boiled too soon
And made my hands so sore
I dropped the cup, the saucer too
And then slipped on the floor.

Under the plaster I'm starting to itch
Around that clapped out knee.
All I can do is bind and bitch
I am so very fed up with me.

By Roma Butcher.

Plain Jane

Big Rory the bully felt puny and small
Dwarfed by young Jane who was slender and tall
When Break-time came Rory yelled at Jane,
"How come you look so strange and so plain?
Steel braces and buck teeth make *you* look a sight
Those mad tufts of hair sometimes give me a fright
Your hands and feet are so huge and flappy
Dress sense is nil, or else it's plain tacky
You're an alien, tell us what planet you're from
Just scoot and get lost, vamoose or be gone."

Five years go by, and now what is this?
Can this vision *be* the same awkward young Miss?
Gliding down catwalk, here comes our Jane
A beautiful model, and no longer plain
Agents go mad to get her on their books
Oozing with class, how haughty she looks
The world is at her designer-clad feet
Completely at ease with celebr'ties she meets.

At Class Reunion they admire her fame
Sharing the glory of this classy dame
Besotted, Big Rory sighs "Jane you're so lovely
How could I ever have thought you were ugly?"
Contented she thinks, "Now life's not so bad"
But remembers the playground where she felt so sad
Yes, sometimes Ducklings can turn into Swans
But sad childhood memories may still linger on.

By Valerie Woollcott

The Cry Of A Lawn Weed.

Hello! Oh! do not look away
You might just tread where I lay.
Look closer, come near to me.
For here lies my family.
This is our home, our community.
I have an Auntie, Uncle and a Granny.

Behold, look at my beauty.
I have a lovely green coat;
And pink and yellow petticoat.
I have been told I am quite cute
And can flutter and dance to suit.

Do look at me, do not look away.
For my hope, my love, my life
This is where I stay.
Have pity, do not weed,
For we have just sown our seed.
We want to live, to love and play.
Do not destroy us, we pray.

By Albertha Braithwaite.

Why Do Angels Gamble?

I can only describe the room in a confused and diffused way. That is how the room was, *is*. That is its purpose. All too real, it is a place only a few have to pass through, and for many of them it is their last. The room is large, and small, light, and dark. It has a smell peculiar to it and it never goes. It has a hushed importance to it. Lights blink, and bottles gurgle, some of the lights make noises, either urgent or reassuringly steady. When the room is big many such flashing lights and lines can be seen, but not understood by those connected to them. Angels with many faces flit from person to person, sometimes staying with one for hours. The room has no colour; it is neutral.

Lights, machines, and Angels are the only distractions. Occasionally there is a panic of lights and noises, and the Angels quietly and calmly rush to and fro. The sounds urgently cry for attention. Only then does consciousness intrude. Is it me? These noises, these alarms of pain? But of course not, if they were I would not know about it. The Angels fuss, and disturbing sounds come from behind the neutral curtains. Sleep again, and then look. The room is bigger now. Open curtains reveal more space, waiting for another. This is a gambler's room, a room that forces decisions no human being should have to face ---- only Angels. The drugs stop you from wondering the odds but afterwards, when you are through it, you wonder why. Why do Angels gamble?

By Simon Butcher

Encounter With Eddie

*J*enny's only encounter with Eddie was a painful one, and of all places it had to be on the level crossing. To make matters worse a fast train was due to pass in less than twenty minutes.

Some time before that she had passed a man in a wheelchair some way back, not giving him a second glance; her mind on other things. Halfway into the crossing a voice shouted from behind, if she could help him release his wheelchair that was stuck on the track. She came face to face with him then as she turned around, noticing at once the knotty stick on his lap. He was studying her face intently.

"I don't know how this has happened. I've crossed here many times over the years and it's the first time I've managed to get my chair stuck." His voice was rough, gravelly.

"Not to worry," she answered, feeling sorry for him, at the same time looking up and down the footpath, but apart from an elderly woman pushing a four wheel shopping trolley, there was no-one else around. Calculating the time quickly while taking in his grubby weather-beaten face, she remarked "There's a train due shortly, so we must hurry. I will try to help as best I can, otherwise we may need to call the Gatekeeper."

She moved nearer, putting her briefcase down, her eyes levelling with his lower half, noticing at once his hands resting on the knotty stick, moving it up and down his knees like a rolling pin. Her brain turned over the possibility that he was acting strangely but she carried on regardless, determined to help him out of his dilemma. Bending down further to examine the wheels she knew at once that the brakes were on. Instead of being stuck on the track the wheelchair was in fact criss-crossed over it. She spoke quickly.

"Will you release your brakes. Your wheelchair doesn't seem to be caught on the line at all. The lines are going the other way. You must have put your brakes on by mistake. Sit back now, and I will push your chair clear so we can get off the crossing."

The flashing lights were now on and the Gatekeeper was patiently waiting for them to pass through the gates before closing them, although the chairbound man had still not released the brakes. She felt an intimidating atmosphere in his presence as she took charge, moving towards the brake handle. Suddenly she felt the full force of something hitting her head, and she realised it was the knotty stick. She scrambled to a kneeling position, dazed, and feeling as if half of her head was missing. He grabbed her hair then, jerking her down towards him, her knees in front of him, his other arm going round her in a neck-lock. She was vaguely aware of people shouting, "Get off the track!" and the Gatekeeper's voice shouting to someone to stop the train, the sound of his footsteps getting nearer and then fading away.

But the man who held her captive was also shouting. "Get away from us or I'll kill her! I mean it!"

Car doors were opening and shutting on both sides of the gates, which were now closed. Dozens of voices were all shouting at the same time. By now his knees were digging into her chest. Everything was becoming a blur as she tried to make sense of it all, focussing her eyes on a heavy-bearded square faced man in his late fifties or so, with wild bloodshot eyes. She gave in to the feeling of faintness, closing her eyes for a few seconds, only to open them with alarm. He had started to shake her viciously; the pain registered on the place on her head where the stick had made it's impact. There was no way she could escape; his grip was far too tight.

"Wake up and listen. I want you in on this before we die," he said sharply, pushing her head back so she had no alternative but to stare him in the face. Something was digging sharply into her neck, and without seeing it she knew it was a knife. Although both her hands were free, she had to use her fingers to grip the wheels for support, but her shoulders were trapped. He continued to shout.

Get back, or she will get this!" The knife left her neck for a few seconds at a time as he waved it at whoever came near. Then back it came, penetrating a new spot in her skin. The pain made her scream out in agony each time. She was also losing her balance, her legs slipping all over the place, her tormented brain trying to make sense of it all.

The gates and the danger of the fast train disappeared from her mind, the pain and fear taking priority over everything until she heard the screeching along the track towards them, and she braced herself for the impact.

"It will soon be over for us" he teased unmercifully. "Can you hear it? It's getting nearer. Can't see it stopping, can you? Even if it stops in time, you will still get this. Yes, I aim to use this on you. That should kill your old man. That's all that matters to me." His bitter words stung the air, loud enough for those who were closest to hear. The noise from the train shrilled louder, drowning out his next words, which were none too genteel. The train stopped suddenly, and the silence that followed seemed to go on forever. It gave her the chance to ask him a question, her trembling voice sounding to her as if it was coming from someone else.

"Why my father? Do you know him? Please tell me, I need to know before I die."

He loosened his grip then, allowing the circulation to move round her body, but it was only a brief respite. Any hope she had of escaping was cut short as he tightened his grip once more, the knife finding another new spot in her neck, and again she let out a scream of agony, seeing the deep hatred in his eyes.

"I know you are one of the Harris girls who live in that big house with all the rich trimmings that should be rightfully mine. Have you heard the story about how your darling Daddy cheated me out of half of my share of the business? The same business that made him a fortune!" He spat out the words with a large dollop of sarcasm in his voice. When she failed to reply, keeping her silence, hoping that he would clarify, he gripped her hair, pushing her head back so that she could smell his whiskey flavoured breath, in order to compel some sort of reply. She obliged.

"I'm Jenny, the eldest. I don't know what you are talking about. Why are you doing this? What have you got against my Daddy? What business? My Daddy has retired. I've taken over the haulage firm. In fact, Daddy gave me half of the business."

Suddenly a movement from behind them distracted her attacker's attention. She heard it as well, and it gave her some sort of hope of escaping from what she could only describe as hell on earth. He jerked his head to one side, shouting to whoever was there to get back double quick and to prove he meant it he dug the knife deeper into her neck. She screamed, her mouth opening and shutting before the words came out.

"Please! Go away! I don't want to die!"

A lot happened after that. The sirens belted out and a helicopter hovered overhead. Then a lot of stamping of feet came near, then faded away. Her captor's demands came loud and clear.

"Get this girl's father. Make it quick, my patience is wearing thin. His name is Peter Harris. Lives two avenues from here. Off Chorale road."

When a male voice asked him for more details of the address, he shouted back in a bitter voice. "Number two, the big house that should be rightfully mine. Tell him I have one of his precious daughters. The dark-haired one."

When he loosened his grip on her shoulders to wave his hand in the air she shouted out. "Don't listen to him! My father has a bad heart. He said he is going to kill me regardless."

She paid dearly for that outburst, the knife moving away from her neck a fraction, finding a new spot, his hand using such force this time that she gasped, choking in shock. Then there was numbness from the neck down, and it was only his strong grip that kept her from subsiding to the ground. Time was now occupied by his screams, his demands, and for the umpteenth time threatening anyone who came as much as a foot nearer. Then he spoke, removing the knife and waving it in the air a few inches from her eyes, mocking her, searching her face.

"Just for you I will go back twenty-eight years. I was just a happy go lucky lad then, enjoying a simple game. Yes, it was just a simple card game, that's all it was at first. I lost my share of the business to your father. I bowed out penniless. The best man won. I took to drinking and within months I lost my lifeline. You see, my lifeline was your mother; she was my girlfriend then, a fragrance of sweetness and I adored her. Yet she chose to marry your father over me. All because I was broke and homeless. I moved away, deeply wounded by my sorrowful loss. I sailed around the world on a cargo ship, trying to forget. Many years passed before I came home, having accumulated a little money to keep me going."

"How did you end up in a wheelchair?" she asked, feeling a rise of sadness. Her father was kindness itself, so she just couldn't imagine him cheating on anyone. But she had to know. Yes, she had to know before she died at the hands of her captor.

"My accident was pure and simple. Self inflicted if you like. Drove my car into a brick wall. Two days before that I overheard a friend of your father's, a man who was at the same card game, telling a female how they had cheated me out of my share of the firm. They both laughed about it. The girl who stood behind me during the game was giving your father a low-down of my cards, and afterwards he rewarded her with a fistful of the money he had stolen from me. I found that out by sheer chance. ten years ago. Ten long years, two of them spent in hospital. Then I found out where your father lived. Yes, he is in for a rude awakening once he knows who I am. Now my revenge is almost over. I believe you are his favourite daughter. Seen you many times with him on your way to the offices where you both work."

She felt trapped like an animal in a snare. Strangely, at this time she felt no fear. She was going to die and in a way she accepted it, guessing it was the only way her mind could handle the whole weird situation. She heard her father's voice asking if she was all right. No words came from her mouth. Her captor was draining every breath from her body and she felt death very near. She now felt sorry for her captor whose eyes bored right through her. A grudge so strong he was embarking on a suicide mission, taking her along with him. She took in the pain showing in his eyes, her lips forming a question, "Are we going to die together?"

He nodded, and she knew. Her father *had* cheated on this man. Robbed him of his life, and in his way, he was doing the same thing. Robbing him of one of his daughters. Her father was now begging for her to be released unharmed. At the same time, begging the man's forgiveness. Promising to put right the wrongs he had done years ago. He repeated this many times, and each time he was met by a barrage of foul words, the knife waving in the air briefly before it made its impact in her neck. She didn't feel it, and she knew she was paralysed. The compassion she felt for her captor was real and forgiving. But it was her father's next words that brought an end to it all.

"Eddie, please forgive me. Take me instead. Not Jenny, please, not Jenny."

"Why not this precious daughter of yours?"

"Look at her Eddie. She is the only one of my girls with dark hair. Can't you guess Eddie?"

"What are you bloody well talking about?"

"She's your daughter Eddie. You are killing *your* daughter."

Jenny recorded this story from her hospital bed. They told her that the paralysis was only temporary and that she would make a full recovery. But she may never recover from the memory of her biological father, who upon hearing who she really was kissed her on the forehead, and smiled for the first and last time. Then he removed the knife gently from her neck, and with deep sadness in his eyes, he plunged it into his heart.

By Mary Ann Naicker

An Unlikely Friendship

Diane awoke with a start from her dozing to Betty's melodious voice calling across the lawn from the old stone wall at the end of garden.

'Where do you think I should put these wallflowers? This bare patch would probably be the best place' she said.

'Wherever you think best, it's no good asking me, you're the gardener. You know that everything I plant just withers away and dies', Diane called back smiling, knowing that whatever she said, Betty would plant wherever she liked. The garden was her domain nowadays, and whatever she put into the ground grew in a profusion of colour and perfume seeming to respond to her constant singing and "plant chatting" as she called it, as if just to please her. Diane stretched in the deckchair and the arthritis, which was plaguing her more frequently these days, slowing her down and restricting her activities considerably, sent a sharp pain down her back making her gasp. The cat, a handsome white Persian, gave a disgruntled hiss and jumped from her lap, stalking off in disgust at the intrusion. In the background she could hear the keys of the old typewriter, tapping away in competition with the sparrows chirruping in the eaves of the old cottage, as her secretary typed the final draft of her novel.

' I really should have got that girl a word processor ages ago, I don't know how she has put up with my antiquated methods all this time; anyway it's too late now because this will be my last book' she thought. `My-last-book` she tested the words slowly out loud to herself, not sure of how she felt about the prospect of not writing again. `Yes` she said determinedly, `It has to be, it is the right time, and it will be the best one yet because it is all true; but no-one will know that except Betty and me. I've hidden it well within the plot and made quite sure of that` she smiled to herself.

Looking across the garden she watched her old friend as her mind drifted back in time to when it all started, so many years ago.

It had been a messy divorce and after much wrangling Diane had ended up with the cottage, the battered old land rover and full custody of Ben, her four year old son. Her errant husband, whose face she could no longer remember had hot-footed it to Spain with his latest nubile and, neither she, nor Ben had ever heard from him again. The income from a trust fund set up by Diane's father had been quite sufficient to keep the wolf from the door, and she had settled down in the small village determined to try and achieve her long buried ambition to become a published writer. Ben had been enrolled at the local school in the town five miles away, where on his first day she had left him, with trepidation, at the school gate. He had looked so small in his oversized blazer and cap, far too young to be away from her all day. Hiding behind a bright smile she had waved at him until he was safely inside, then walked slowly back to the car. At home she had restlessly wandered around the house from room to room, drank endless cups of coffee, dusted and re-dusted the furniture, and roamed the garden, aimlessly pulling out weeds that turned out not to be weeds after all. When it was time to collect him she had arrived at the school far too early, and then eagerly scanned the little faces of the children lazily walking out of the school gate, searching for her boy.

'Hi Mum' his voice shouted behind her. 'This is my new friend Joe, we have the same birthday!'

Diane spun around at the sound of his voice and looked into the shiniest, blackest face, and darkest brown eyes she had ever seen; a complete contrast to the golden hair and bright blue eyes of her son.

'Oh! Hello Joe, I'm very pleased to meet you`, she said slightly flustered, then added quickly, trying to hide her surprise 'Are you waiting for your mother? `

Just then a voice, very out of breath and with an anxious tone called from behind her.

`Joseph! Joe! Oh there you are! I'm sorry I'm a bit late, I was held up at the hospital`, the voice said with relief. Diane turned and met the dazzling smile of a handsome, statuesque Jamaican woman dressed in a nurse's uniform.

`How do you do? `, the woman said. ` I'm Betty White, Joe's mother.`

After self-conscious introductions were made the two women turned towards their offspring, whose arms were draped around each others shoulders both beaming broadly.

`We have a joke for you`, they said in unison. ` We want to know why? `.

` Why what?` Diane said, glancing quizzically at the other woman.

`Well` giggled Ben, `my name is Black, and I am a white boy`.

`And my name is White and I am a black boy`, echoed Joe.

For a long moment neither woman spoke, and then simultaneously they looked at each other and collapsed into helpless laughter, to the extreme delight of the two boys. Smiling at the memory, Diane pulled herself out of her reverie and forced her mind to focus on the present.

`That was the day when it all began`, she remembered. `Two single mothers from different backgrounds, social class, financial status, religion and race; rearing sons with the same seemingly insurmountable differences.   Myself, a privileged child from white middle class parents, with the benefit of a private school education. Ultimately, disappointing my parents by marrying a "good for nothing" womaniser`. Diane's thoughts were racing now. `Then there was Betty, from poverty stricken parents in the slums of Jamaica, having been sent to England to live with relatives at twelve years old, primarily to be educated. Only to be used by them as an unpaid servant, until she left school and set about educating herself, finally achieving her nursing qualifications; also, upsetting her family, by refusing to get married at all. It was all so long ago, where did all the years go? ` sighed Diane. `How did we get to be so old? `

She watched her friend dead-heading the roses, and noticed for the first time how slow her movements had become, how her hair was getting greyer by the day and her bearing, now slightly stooped, not quite as erect as it had once been.

` I owe all my success to her friendship` Diane mused, `I couldn't have got through any of it without her support`.The typewriter keys had stopped their tapping and Diane guessed that her secretary was preparing to leave for the day. The sun was low in the sky now, and long dark shadows were stealthily creeping across the lawn like black phantoms. The birdsong had stopped and the crackling evening chorus of the crickets had taken its place.

`I've nearly finished, ten more minutes and I'll make us some supper`, called Betty.

A sharp breeze swept across the garden causing Diane to feel a chill, she pulled her cashmere wrap closely around her as her memory jumped back to a time that had destroyed one friendship, but had cemented another which had lasted for half a lifetime. She tried to resist the painful memories that were flooding back, but in the eerie, ghostlike quality of the early evening light which was shrouding the garden, she seemed to have no control over her thoughts and the years rolled away.

Diane sat in the chapel staring straight ahead, seeing nothing but the coffin, not believing this could be happening. Somewhere in the back of her conscious mind she was aware of the soft murmur and shuffling of people arriving, filling up the rows of wooden pews that ran down each side of the narrow aisle in the small country church. She only half registered their careful footfalls as they tried hard not to make a sound on the flag-stoned floor as everyone self-consciously tried to find a seat. The heavy, sickly scent of lilies and incense permeated the air, and a red shaft of sunlight from the stained glass window danced on the coffin like a firefly; the union flag which was draped over it fluttering in the breeze each time the chapel door opened. It was as though she was watching the scene from the opposite end of binoculars; seeing herself from some far off place, looking at a stranger. Diane forced herself to turn her head and her gaze rested on the young man sitting in the front pew on the opposite side of the church.

`How smart he looks in his uniform, all brushed up and shiny` she thought. ` Just as I remember him when he was a child`. The next thought almost tore her heart from her breast and she felt her breathing becoming restricted.

`But, there is someone missing; and now he will always be missing`, she squeezed her eyes shut and tried to blot out the reality of the scene around her, but the tears which she had thought were all cried out, had started again.

Joe had sat with his head bowed down since arriving at the chapel; his fists were clenched on his knees and his body tense with barely suppressed anger and helplessness. Devastation and grief were etched clearly in his face and filling his eyes. She suddenly realised that they had been closer than brothers from kindergarten to University; and later into the Armed Forces. After Sandhurst they had both been posted to the Gulf, to that cruel, and God forsaken desert wasteland that had taken her beloved boy, changing all their lives forever. Her eyes moved to the woman sitting next to him, her usual laughing face was a mask of pain. Her statuesque figure seemed somehow diminished, as though something substantial had been removed and had left a husk, empty and crushed. Her hand was clasped tightly around a posy of red and white flowers, her fingers absently pulling at the petals which dropped unnoticed to the floor. Ben had loved her, calling her Mummy B from a very early age, a pet name that had stuck into adulthood. Diane wanted to move across the aisle and sit with her friend so they would be able to give and take comfort from each other. She didn't want to sit feeling alone, surrounded by distant family who she hardly ever saw, or by the military dignitaries spouting empty words of condolence, and who, in her unbearable grief she held responsible for her son's death. With sudden clarity Diane realised that Betty had loved Ben as much as she loved her own son, and her pain was as great as Diane's. In despair and uncontrollable rage she felt the bitterness rise from her chest to her throat, and explode in the tormented wail of an injured animal, reverberating off the stone walls of the chapel; then, merciful, comforting blackness. Diane remembered nothing else from that day, or from the months that followed, except for the smiling, black face, which was always there, looking down at her as she swam in and out of consciousness, heavily sedated, and engulfed in depression and grief; not wanting to emerge from under the dark and comforting blanket of oblivion. The long road back from that desperate place had been through her writing, and with the support of her remarkable friend she had eventually become well again.

Diane wrapped her arms around herself and shivered violently, not sure whether the sudden chill was from her recollections of that terrible time, or from the damp evening air. Betty's cheery voice brought her thankfully back to the safety of the present.

`There, that's all the planting finished, now we'll have some tea`. `Oh, you're shivering, have you been day-dreaming again? ` she admonished, wagging her finger. `Come on now lets go in, and I'll start our supper` she said.

`I'll be along in a moment` Diane replied, watching, with deep affection, her dearest friend walk slowly back to the house, calling the dogs for their supper as she went.

Taking a last stroll around the garden in the fast fading light, Diane stopped in front of the side gate which led into the country lane. Her eyes lingered on the archway above the gate which was laden with roses of dark red, almost black blooms, intermingling with bright, delicate, snowy white blossoms of African Vine, their scent heady and overpowering in the evening air. She remembered the day Ben and Joe had planted the bushes, neither boy believing that the bare leafless sticks they were carefully putting into the ground, under Betty's strict instructions, would grow into anything at all, let alone the heavy mass of flowers that was threatening the archway with collapse today.

`These bushes are like us and our lives` she thought. `Completely different in appearance and origin, but living and growing together in harmony. We have overcome so much prejudice and opposition over the years due to our friendship, from all kinds of sources; some veiled and surreptitious, and some downright blatant and vindictive` the last thought making her angry.

Shaking the thoughts away, Diane plucked one of each of the blossoms and walked slowly back into the house. The sound of Betty in full voice, singing along with the radio, brought a smile to her lips.

`By the way, Joe is coming tomorrow, and he's bringing the little ones` Betty shouted from the kitchen, in mid-song.

`That's wonderful, Betty, I'll make some cakes for the children`, Diane called back, her spirit lifting.

As she passed her study door Diane saw the finished manuscript lying on her desk. Picking it up she sat down in her favourite old armchair and leafed through the heavy sheaf of papers. Her eyes wandered over the bookshelves and stopped at the row of novels that were her own.

`Yes` she thought, `this will be my last book, and the best one yet, a kind of epitaph to one unlikely friendship, borne out of the unlikely friendship of two small boys.`

By Patricia Barber

I Know My Place

Chapter One --- Lucy

I feel as if I am standing on top of the world. The sun is a dazzling white eye in a cloudless azure sky. We are so high that despite the searing heat there is a delicious breeze. From my vantage point on top of the bell tower the scene below looks like a painting.

Robert hands me his telescope. I can see the grounds of Blackthorn Manor. To the right there are the stables, the Maze, the Kitchen Garden, and Mother's pride and joy, her Rose Garden. I can also see our own small Church. To the front I can see the long wide road leading up to the entrance gates. It is flanked by tall stately poplars. To the left our meadows, orchards and woods. Beyond the grounds I see smoke curling from the Pottery chimneys. Close by are the two Inns, and the Village Church. I can see the stream that runs between the cottages, and the Forge. Even further away are the farms that are part of the Estate.

Blackthorn Manor has stood for centuries, proud and high on the brow of the hill, a landmark that can be seen from miles away. Apart from the Pottery and the Inns, everything belongs to father. Robert is the eldest son, and one day he will be the next Lord Davenport. I am ten years old, the baby of the family.

"Right, climb down Lucy," says Robert, "it's time for your French and Latin lessons with the très jolie Mademoiselle Devoux." I like Mlle Devoux. She is indeed very pretty. She insists that we converse only in French. We often take our lessons in the gardens. Sometimes, mostly when we are out riding, she describes Paris to me. It sounds such an exciting city. Her mother who still lives there sometimes sends her dress patterns, and mother lets our Dressmaker use them. Très chic!

I hate Arithmetic and English lessons. Miss Black lives up to her name. She always wears black, has a face that looks like she is sucking lemons, and is very strict. I think she is very old, she is certainly very deaf.

"Lucy!" she shouts. "Where are you child? Now walk, don't run!" I often hide from her which is easy because I can smell the chalk and dust from her gowns. And I hear her stick tip-tapping as she walks down the corridors.

I enjoy my piano lessons. Mr Johns says that music is the food of the soul, and I believe him. If I feel very sad I play happy country tunes, and sometimes the younger maids will dance comically around the piano, and we finish up laughing. I may have to do that tonight as Mama and I are visiting some poor folk today. We went into the attic and found some old toys. There was a doll, some lead soldiers, a ball, a spinning top, a hoop and some children's books. Hopefully these items, along with some sweetmeats and fruit from our Orangery will bring them a little cheer. We are visiting three families in all, but I think the last is the saddest. The mother recently died in childbirth, and the baby boy was stillborn. I think the poor man has several other young children.

The ride from the Manor has been exhilarating. Mother took the pony and trap. So much more fun than stuffy enclosed carriages. The cow parsley is high in the hedgerows, it looks like lacy, creamy parasols. We watch the Bee Keepers gathering the clover honey, and the sheep-dogs rounding up their fat, fluffy flock.

As we pull up at the last cottage a little girl of seven years or so rushes out. Bobbing several curtsies she says, "Welcome Lady Alice, Lady Lucy, please come and see our new ducklings." Jabbering non-stop she leads us to a small duck-pond. She gives us some bread;

"Would you like to feed them?"

A tall thin girl appears.

"I'm sorry Miladies, Kate is such a chatterbox. Please to come in and meet the rest of the family."

It takes a while for our eyes to adjust to the gloom inside the cottage. So many eyes are upon us. There is a pungent smell of cabbage combined with wood smoke. Hanging from every corner are bunches of greenery. Shelf upon shelf of jars and pots. There are so many children to be crowded into such a tiny room. Who on earth will look after them now that their mother has gone?

****

Chapter Two --- Hope

I have cleaned the cottage and changed the blankets on the beds, and tidied the shelves as best I can. The children are dressed in their Sunday best, and I have charged Kate with keeping them presentable. The little ones have been bribed with cake and apples to make then stay indoors. A kind neighbour has lent me two china cups, and I have made two sponge cakes. The cocoa is ready to make hot chocolate for Lady Alice and her daughter.

It has been two weeks since the funerals of mother and baby Joseph. Thank heavens dear Mama taught Martha and I her secrets. In the traditions of her calling mother passed to her eldest daughters the art of harvesting the herbs and wild plants, how to grind with mortar and pestle, and to sort them and blend them into potions and lotions. Folk still come from miles around to buy our remedies.

People tell me that I look like my mother. I am ten years old, the eldest of seven children. Unfortunately I am as yet too young to have mastered mother's other skills. Mayhap as I get older it will come. In the past I have watched folk enter our cottage tense and hunched, sometimes even tearful, laden down with their woes. And most of them, after confiding their problems and then listening to mother's soft country voice, went back down the lane as if a black cloud had blown away. She had a rare gift that not many possess.

At first after mother died I wondered how we would live without her laughter, gentleness, and wisdom. However, we *are* surviving. I have had to sacrifice my schooling to look after the children and carry on mother's trade, so I have little time to grieve. Father's wages from the Pottery pay the rent, most of the rest goes to the Landlord at The Fisherman's Arms. Pa is friendly with Bill the poacher, so he sometimes brings home rabbits, trout, and game. Once, as a rare treat, we had a joint of venison. In return for these favours Pa keeps a lookout and helps him carry his spoils. Pa says that Bill has the eyes of an eagle, the ears of a fox, the memory of an elephant, and is as quick as a field mouse.

We keep our own hens and ducks, and we have apple and plum trees. I am also tending mother's vegetable patch. There are many other poor people worse off than us.

A large bluebottle buzzes angrily in and out of the reed roof and I yell, "Quick Martha, jump on the table and swat it! What's that smell? Oh no, the baby needs changing again! Listen! I can hear a pony and trap coming! Kate, run outside to greet them, and keep them talking as long as you can. And don't forget to curtsy!"

By Valerie Woollcott

The Butterfly And The Bench.

Hello there!
Hello there I say!
You, sitting there! You're in my way.
What a silly place to be-
In front of this cemetery.
In this position;
What is your mission?
Tell me I pray.

But, speak softly – do not disturb
Those who lie here in rows so neat,
Such an orderly display.

Little bench are you not afraid?
As in the dark they talk all night;
And gossip of things that are gone.
Each with a ghostly story to tell –
Tales that make your hair rise.
A midnight sound – the creak and groan.
Of bodies festering, empty eyes that gaze.

Little bench, I'll bid you goodbye.
Though comfortable this seat, I'll not bide.
But, bid you farewell.
For I seek a brighter world – where no-one creeps.

By Albertha Braithwaite

A Story Of Wining Women And Boring Men.

There, it was done. Enough to kill an army, the tablets crushed and mixed in a sauce with chillies and hot peppers. He enjoys spicy food. She placed the dish precisely in the centre of the oven, checked timer and temperature and closed the door with a slight smile.

Time for a glass of wine or two. Time to reflect on the past three years, such boring years. Her husband was a man addicted to the comforts of home - and television. Addicted wasn't too strong a word, she had been able to pry him out of his shelter for just one expensive dinner in town and one fairly luxurious week-end only. He had complained all the time, missing his favourite quiz programmes, his sport and, of course, his comfortable armchair.

'Don't ask me again' he had said, 'I like my week-ends at home.' As for the meal out, well wouldn't you know my cooking was far more interesting. Yes, well tonight's meal would probably be that.

She poured another glass of wine. Men really were very difficult to live with.

Her first husband, young, brash, barely an adult really had become tiresome in his reckless pursuit of new adventures. He'd spent far too much of her money before she realised that it would be quite easy to be rid of him. No-one was surprised when he para-glided straight into a cliff while holidaying in the South of France. No-one asked too many questions of the distraught young widow who sobbed and sobbed until after his funeral.

She refilled her glass.

After a decent interval she moved north and soon joined the 'smart set' in her chosen city. She met her second husband at the races. Considerably older than herself, with a solidly successful business, he was a no frills Yorkshireman and very shortly, a total turn off. He worked long hours for six days a week and on the seventh, Sundays, he filled the beautiful house with a loud, hard drinking racing crowd. For a while she tried to fit in but was never comfortable with his friends, nor they with her. She realised also that he bet large sums of money on horse races all over the country every day. She grew to thoroughly dislike him, his friends, and, more importantly, his betting. How much did he lose? How much money did he actually have left?

He was a little more difficult to dispose of. An unfortunate accident on the cellar steps, he was carrying too many bottles and had been drinking. Her story was accepted. A large house, herself upstairs in the bedroom watching television, she heard nothing. She found him in the morning and was suitably upset.

In her present reflective mood she had to admit a faint feeling of guilt.

She had more wine as she remembered the rather hurried move from Yorkshire to London, seeking perhaps a little culture? A few theatres, concerts and the like, in congenial company of course - and what did she find but the most boring man on the whole planet. She giggled a little as she thought of him, he simply had no class. Actually, now she realised that he was also late home from his office in the Ministry, too.

Goodness, might as well finish this bottle, now, open another one for him. She laughed, stumbling a little as she turned the oven down to 'low'. Whoa, she thought, you're drunk. Oh well, why not, this was a special occasion.

The telephone rang. No greeting, he simply told her that he would not be coming home, tonight or ever again, he had moved in with his lover and his solicitor would be in touch. Good-bye.

She walked slowly into the kitchen and took the dish from the oven, realising that she was hungry. It was good, hot and spicy.

By Roma Butcher.

The First Time

(A young girl's lament)

"My God," she thought sadly, "is that all?
I really thought the sky would fall
Instead I'm feeling I could choke
It seems he's just another bloke.

It's great my magazines all stated
How sad it turned out overrated
If only he had held me tight
And snuggled close all through the night

He's had his way and now he's sleeping
Tho' eyes are dry, inside I'm weeping
He's turned away, ignoring me,
His hairy back is all I see

My innocence he had to steal
Oblivious to how I feel
Off he'll swagger in the morning
I should have heard the Gypsy's warning

Will I ever know the glory
That I read in every story?
Man and Woman joined in bliss?
Or will it always be like this?

By Bill Davies

(Runner-up in Writers Forum
Poetry Competition November 2007)

The Sea

Skies weep salt of human tears
Distant thunder loud and deep
Echo the heartache of distress
As years pound the shore
Vomiting wreckage of lost love
The pain of life ebbing and flowing
Emptying the barren beach

Winds pierce from the East
Dark clouds lie heavy in the sky
Ready to disperse their fleecy contents
Orange sun disappears behind the gathering storm
Quietly the white shower descends to earth
Slowly at first, then larger flakes fall
Faster onto the waiting ground
Draping the landscape in its winter robes
Crystals sparkle the earth pure, untouched
Footprints become frozen in time
A soft white world iglooed in silence
'Til a waiting sun cracks its winter shell.

By Pamela Harris

The Tramp

I may have chosen this life as a vagrant, which is filled with solitude, but I still like talking to people. I don't mean close relationships or intimate communication. I left all that behind me long ago. As it's Autumn now, I am heading towards London. Billy says it's going to be a hard Winter, and the city does have the soup runs and sleeping places for most of us. I usually fare all right in London. The crowd I usually meet call me 'The Prof' or 'The Gent,' because I speak fairly well.

I am a good listener if they want to stay sober and talk, but I've told them nothing about my past.

I always make a point of taking this road, though it makes the journey longer, but if I'm lucky I'll see *her*. The house is a bit isolated, and surrounded by tall trees. Last time I saw her, she didn't look too happy, so I'd like to spend a little time checking up on her. As I neared her home I could hear the television. Hiding behind the trees, I had a good view through the kitchen window. The light was on and she was working at the sink. She turned away and poured beer into a pint glass and took it into the sitting room. Almost immediately she returned to the kitchen. She began cleaning the crockery, clearing and tidying as she went. When finished, she sat for a moment drying her hands. Within seconds, he called her to come through to him. Wiping her brow, she turned out the light and disappeared. I propped myself up against a tree, deciding to stay until morning, in the hope of seeing more of her. The mildness of the evening meant that I'd be in some comfort.

Sleep doesn't come quickly. It never does when I stop here. Old memories force their way through. Walking through the trees, holding her hand. Singing songs slowly with her, until she learned the words. This part of my life was happy, until the day I learned of my wife's affair. It had been going on for years. She had known him from her school days. He had refused to consider marriage; I had been her second choice. The deception had proved too much for me so I'd packed a bag and left. It was the day I most regretted.

Through the years I returned secretively to check how things were. My wife eventually moved away leaving my now grown-up daughter alone. I watched as she blossomed and met her future partner. I visited regularly, but kept my anonymity. She never knew I was there, except for one occasion when we accidentally met on the road.

"Good morning madam," I said, taking off my hat. "Lovely day."

She just smiled and walked on. With this thought to comfort me I lapsed into sleep.

I was suddenly startled awake by her screams. Jumping up, I ran as fast as I could through the open door. He was standing over her, the belt in his hand, striking her repeatedly. I snatched it from him and struck him hard a few times. He fell to the floor then turned and stared at me, blood dripping from his nose.

"Who the hell are you?" he shouted.

"That doesn't matter," I shouted back. "You were beating this young lady ... I heard her screams." She sat up slowly.

"Thank you so much. -- God knows what might have happened. Are you a neighbour? I think I've seen you before."

Being this close I could see old fading bruises, and fresh weals smeared with blood. Without hesitation I said, "No, I was just passing."

The man sat on the floor looking dazed. I said to her, "Are you going to call the police? I presume you are going to charge him."

"When he gets drunk it changes him and he gets violent." She paused for quite a while. "I do think I need to get help before it's too late."

After phoning the police she turned to me and asked, "What's your name?"

"It's John," I answered, "I'll stay with you until they come."

As soon as I heard the police car approaching I slipped out of the house. I watched as the car took them both away.

It was some time before I saw her again. She told me later that she had gone into a refuge until he was no longer a threat. Though I see her every six months, I never disclose that I am her father. I am just the friendly tramp, who is now a regular visitor.

It's better that way.

By Chris Lammas.

Old Fashioned Love.

Sixty years, a lifetime say some,
confined in a marshmallow prison.
Unbreakable bars of bitter-sweet candy;
yet soft, so they melt in the sun.

Shackled together with gossamer ties;
close - so close, but never touching.
A smile with a whisper, a knowing glance;
harsh words are few, so too are cruel lies.

Milestones glitter for a day, then go;
Silver, Ruby, Gold, and Diamond.
Years merge together as though they are one,
like an evening tide in its ebb and flow.

Old worn in slippers facing each other,
across a hearthrug faded with age.
Needles clicking, the radio low;
a newspaper rustles, ` Some cocoa Mother? `

The pattern book is marked with a pen;
knitting bundled into a canvas bag.
High on a shelf is a sepia `snap`
of a wartime bride, `How young we were then.`

Closely woven each heart and mind,
with bright silks of memories, in the twilight years.
An intricate pattern of comforting sameness
knits two together; forever entwined.

By Patricia Barber

The Good Wife.

He was very quiet this morning, moving deliberately and not speaking. She asked if his breakfast was alright, egg yolks the right consistency, toast brown but soft and she hated herself for this. He hadn't the grace to answer and left the house quietly, closing the front door gently. She watched him as he strode to the garage, looking tall and distinguished, brown hair gleaming in the morning sun. Impeccably dressed as always.

As she cleared away and washed the dishes she could feel her muscles tightening. She was trying to move soundlessly though she could never understand her need for silence when he was out.

After tidying the spotless, shining, soulless house she mowed the lawns, looked for weeds in the immaculate flower beds and trimmed the boxed hedge. She wasn't hungry but forced herself to have soup. She prepared supper then sat in the shady garden watching birds and insects going about their business.

It was quiet and peaceful this summer afternoon but she couldn't rest, eager to have the perfect meal cooked perfectly for him, anticipating his return. She showered and changed, putting on his favourite dress. Making up carefully she brushed her blonde hair to fall softly around her shoulders.

Early evening and she went to the hall to greet him. He handed her his briefcase, smiling. He poured wine for them both, drank his quickly before going upstairs to change while she put supper on the table. A traditional dining room, dark furniture polished to a satin sheen, silver on the sideboard, fine napery.

She refilled his glass and handed it to him. He laughed and sat down to eat. She picked at her food as he stared at her across the table. She put down her knife and fork as he stood up, reaching for her plate and smashing it over her head. A mixture of warm blood and food ran down her face.

The beating was swift and savage, both of them silent throughout. The broken plate had pierced her skin in several places and she thought of her dress being torn. With a final kick to her face he moved away.

After a time she went upstairs, slowly, into the bathroom and locked the door. For a few minutes she sat on the edge of the bath willing herself to keep calm, not to dwell on this latest abuse. The beatings were becoming more frequent and he had never before kicked her face.

She took off her stained clothes as she ran a hot bath. Looking into the mirror she saw that the cut on her head had stopped bleeding and her hair would cover the bruised cheek. Lowering her aching body into the water she swore, again, that this would be the last.

Much later, when she went down to make a hot drink she realised the house was empty. He must have walked to his local for a relaxing drink she thought grimly.

Hours later she was awakened by the insistent ringing of the bedside telephone. It was the local hospital. They were sorry, they said, but could she come down right away, her husband had been found in the street. It was a stroke, quite severe.

The weeks passed. She tended the garden every morning, her mind closed, visiting him in the afternoons. He recognised her but could not speak. She broke the silence only to chat with nurses as they made him comfortable.

When the time came hospital staff explained that they needed his bed and queried her ability to look after him, suggesting a nursing home. She assured them she would be able to manage. Her eyes locked on his as she said 'Oh yes, really, I'll be happy to, I know exactly what he needs.

By Roma Butcher.

Spring

A golden patch of aconites bright,
Cheerful in the morning light
Virginal snowdrops nodding white heads
Like drifts of snow in brown earth beds
Primulas glowing in every hue
Posies of colour so fresh and so new
Catkins rustling high on the trees
Like lambs tails waving in the gentle breeze
Confetti blossoms falling pink and white
Carpet the ground, what a pretty sight
Daffodils dancing in a perfect ring
All Nature's rejoicing, at last it's Spring!

By Valerie Woollcott

The Monster

The Monster awoke. She felt strange. One moment there had been total oblivion, and then, for no apparent reason, she had become aware and capable of thought. She looked down at her black shiny body, and as she observed the tiny forms of human beings gazing up at her, she realised how big she was. "I wonder if I can move?" she thought. Experimentally she flexed one of the three bulbous fingers of her right hand. She sensed movement, and encouraged by this she tried to lift her arm.

A little family were standing at the south side of The Millennium Bridge or the Wobbly Bridge as some sceptics had dubbed it. They were gazing at the various sights, the London Eye, St Paul's Cathedral on the north side of the bridge, Shakespeare's Globe Theatre, The Festival Hall, and Tower Bridge, some distance down river. The father, in a rather pompous way, was commenting at large on all the famous landmarks. A small hand tugged at his coat tails to get his attention, and when he looked, the hand pointed. His son was looking at the Tate Modern Art Gallery and the strange modern sculpture standing in front of it.

"Hmmm," said Dad. "Ugly looking brute, isn't it? Well, it is supposed to be a work of art my son, but it's not really my cup of tea. They do display some rubbish as works of art don't they Mavis?" He looked at his wife, expecting her to agree, but she just turned her eyes to the sky and tut-tutted. The small hand tugged again, and as he looked down he was shocked to see that the little boy's eyes were as big as saucers, and his jaw agape. He followed the boy's eyes, and immediately his face took on the same expression.

The sculpture had moved! The arm had been raised, and one finger was scratching the huge black shiny head. There were a few screams from the watching crowd, but most believed that it was a stunt, and that the arm was raised by mechanical means. When the Monster stood up, snapping it's anchoring steel cables as if they were silk threads, pandemonium broke out. The Wobbly

Bridge lived up to its name as hundreds of panicking sightseers fled northwards. The pompous Dad led the way.

The Monster lifted one huge globe-like foot, and then lifted the second; elated, she placed one in front of the other. She could walk! ---- She moved ponderously towards the river bank, people scurrying out of her way in all directions. One elderly man was too slow, and a huge foot enveloped him. As it rose again the poor man re-appeared, frozen with fear, bur unharmed. As she was an inflatable she was in effect as light as air, and he hadn't been crushed.

She waded out into the river and sat in the water, using her huge hands to propel herself along. She seemed compelled to approach the Houses of Parliament, and drifted toward Westminster Bridge. River traffic veered to either side of her, but curiously there was no attempt made to stop her. She made her way to the north bank just below the bridge, and clambered out. Motor vehicles driving beside the embankment screeched to a halt as the huge form lumbered across the road.

Parliament Square was already in chaos, several hundred people, some with placards, were demonstrating outside the Palace of Westminster. There were Trade Union banners, and banners from a number of motoring organisations. Dozens of big lorries had parked all around the Square and the drivers were honking their horns. The blue line of Policemen restraining the crowd fell back, but held firm.

The Monster stopped in front of the gates, placed her hands on her hips, lifted her head, and a voice, distinctly feminine, called out "Power to the people!" The crowd were delighted, and a ragged cheer went up. --- Here was a powerful ally! One young woman with long red hair looked up wonderingly. She was wearing overalls and was carrying a placard which proclaimed, **'New Road Taxes Unfair to Women Lorry Drivers!'**

She turned to her companion and said, "Wow! She's a real big Bertha!"

The Monster heard this, and thought, "Big Bertha! I like that. Yes, Big Bertha it shall be!" ---- She had a name.

Bertha looked at all the placards and was amazed to discover that she could read. She saw that the crowd were protesting about the proposal to tax motor vehicles by putting 'Spy' boxes in them, and she finally understood why she had been animated. ---- It was so that she could support motorists, life-blood of the country's Motorway arteries. She crouched down, stroking her chin, and in a conspiratorial whisper she asked the redhead "What's the plan?"

The girl shrugged. "We wanted to see Tony Blair. --- We have a petition with half a million signatures of people who don't agree with the Government's plans. -- We want to present it to the Prime Minister personally, but he won't speak to us."

"Won't he," said Bertha grimly. "We'll see about that." The strange impelling force came over her again, and she made her way back to the river, stepping over people and vehicles deftly, and slipped back into the water, this time above the bridge.

She drifted up river until she reached the members terrace. She could hear the clink of teacups and the fruity sound of whisky being poured. She moved towards a group of distinguished looking people.

The Prime Minister was just about to down a wee dram when this huge cubic head appeared above the railings. The long nose jutted towards him menacingly. almost pushing him off his chair.

"Tony Blair," came the Monster's voice, "what is your worst nightmare?"

He blinked. "Well, up to now, I thought it was Gordon Brown taking over as Leader."

"Silly boy," purred Bertha, "let me enlighten you." And she leaned towards him, pulled her nose to one side, and whispered into his ear.

The Prime Minister turned white, his knees began to shake, and he said, "Yes Bertha! Right away Bertha!" He leaned across the table to the portly figure of his Deputy, and shouted, "Wake up John!" As Mr Prescott opened his bleary eyes Mr Blair shouted, "Quick John, send somebody to bring those Motoring representatives in here! I'm having second thoughts about those Road Tax proposals!" Mr Prescott trotted off, and Mr Blair looked fearfully around at Bertha.

She winked, and patted his shoulder. "Good lad," she said approvingly, "I knew you'd see sense."

She stepped back into the river, laid down on her back with her hands behind her head, and let the current carry her down river. A triumphant fanfare of lorry horns rang out a salute. As she drifted slowly along, she wondered idly if they would open Tower Bridge for her.

By Bill Davies

Childhood Memories

The air expectant. Tension crackling like lightning as two urchin gangs faced each other at the side of the local pond. Ducks, already aware that something was about to happen, circled cautiously. Slowly emerging from a pathway of trampled bushes and broken trees, boys of various ages appeared, socks down, knees dirty from kneeling, all of them carrying bits of wood, tin cans, string hanging from pockets. Girls standing by the grassy banks to cheer and support their brothers and friends.

For this was the day of the great raft race, when two rival teams vied for supremacy. Their task was to assemble from scratch a floatable raft to cross from one bank to another. Out of the jumpers and jackets came pieces of rope and wire taken from Dad's shed, to be used to tie various struts together. The raft to be completed on the bankside. Pulled from adjacent undergrowth, secretly hidden from the other team, came oil drums for buoyancy, fence palings and sundry pieces of wood to be tied together with anything that had any length to it. Ties and braces for lashing were contributed by various youths to help their side to win. Each team trying to plunder goods from each other. Tempers fraying as things went wrong or did not work out.

They were fortified with paste and jam sandwiches, washed down with bottles of water.

The morning passed as two indescribable, weird and wonderful, hopefully floatable vessels were constructed. With great pride both gangs pushed and pulled their boats over stones and mud into green water. Each eyeing up the other team's efforts. With tentative steps a plimsolled boy stepped onto the crazy paving boards, holding on to broom-handle mast, getting a balance before the next lad attempted to board. Grubby white handkerchiefs fluttered as the rafts were launched across choppy waters, hands, fingers, and cricket bats paddling frantically to speed progress. Both boats veering together before being clumsily pushed apart by angry participants.

The race head to head before one, weighted down with water, began to sink. Tin cans were used as buckets to bale out excess water. The crew, seeing the inevitable, jumped overboard into waist-high water. Once tied planks broke free, floating away into the path of the soon to be victorious craft. The delight of the winners boundless, excited cries of success echoed across the countryside.

The defeated team clambered up the riverbank, wet, dirty, and defeated, already with a plan in their heads for the next year.

Childhood at its best, remembered with affection by us would-be sailors.

By Pamela Harris

Prize Winner at the Frinton Literary Festival
Short Story Competition 2006

Space

The space is filled with wood and cloth and air and it moves with me. It can take me wherever I want. Self-contained, calm or fast, safe or riotously dangerous, it is a home and a vehicle. It is of course my boat.

I step onto the boat, *his* space. Sleek and solid, yet it moves easily with my weight, accepting me. I look around, catching glimpses of him. - Binoculars not put away properly, half-empty tea-mug from his last adventure. His tidy tardiness. Wind rips through the sheets and I know what he means. The noise sings, "Take me! Use me! -- I'll keep you safe!"

I visualise him. -- That look of total completeness that I wish *I* could give him. I should hate this boat, but it makes him happy. It doesn't compete with me. -- He made us both. I touch the brass railings, feeling their strength, *his* strength. Together we will keep him safe.

I look around the cabin. Solid, good polished wood. Even his untidy ways can't disturb the symmetry of construction. Deep inside the boat it still exudes a confidence. ---

"I am built to last. I will always be here." -- Like him.

All the wood is polished. Not by him, he doesn't 'do' polish, but by the boatyard - polished to last, professionally. I move to the forward bunks, our bunks. It's different in here. Rough wood is patched over the starboard bow, destroying the symmetry of the cabin. I can't face this and go back on deck.

I sit in the cockpit and look forward. *He* is there - standing in the bow like 'Titanic' but facing me. He stands. --- Long legs astride, braced for the non-existent waves, holding the jib-sheet, face brown, and smiling at me. He looks fit and strong in his T-shirt and jeans and smiles again and says *"I love you."* I'm about to tell him I love him when the voice of the boatyard owner Peter breaks the silence.

"I'm so sorry Mrs Bell. I've come to look at the damage."

Peter is in the Yacht Club launch, his heavy Essex accent kindly and reassuring. I help him tie up on the port side and he comes aboard. *He* is gone now, but I think Peter and I both know he's still around. He wants us to know what happened and as we look at the caved-in starboard hull we can only guess for now --- but we will find out. For *his* sake. --- For mine.

By Simon Butcher

Antique

What do I do with this antique?
Sitting on my window sill,
Weekly dusting year in, year out,
An ugly, gleaming monstrosity.

What do I do with this antique?
Passed down to me years ago,
The silent figurine with piercing eyes,
With flowing dark brown cloak.

What do I do with this antique?
Majestic in its day.
A flat square hat sitting on his head;
A candle glow lights up his face.

What do I do with this antique?
The judge with the piercing eyes.
Long ago, his flat hat on show,
The gallows takes a life.

What do I do with this antique?
With duster in my hand,
Unsteady movement, with just a slip,
Problems solved; shattered pieces where I stand.

By Mary Ann Naicker.

Flying The Nest

I recently watched an episode of Bill Oddie's Spring Watch. I watched with amusement as a last fledgling struggled with leaving the nesting box. The final flight that led him to the outside world seemed to daunt him. Occasionally he fluttered to the opening hole, and teetered on the edge. Several times he lost his nerve and returned to the safety of the box.

I had only one fledgling left at home. From the age of sixteen my son had quite a few friends, and had also acquired a few short-term girlfriends. Most of the time he enjoyed being part of a group of young people close to home. We welcomed all of them into our home, and it became a regular meeting place. My husband and I got to know them all very well, and liked the house being full of fun. At first our son worked locally, but his second job was working for the Treasury, which is based in the centre of London. We watched as he developed from a teenage boy into a confident young man.

One quiet evening he came into the kitchen as I washed up and picked up the tea towel. --- Which was most unusual.

I know now that he wanted to talk, but needed the distraction of a task, which meant that he could avoid my eyes.

"Mum, you know we had a Christmas party at work? Well, I met this girl there, and she's been popping in and out of my office ever since. ------ I think she likes me."

"Well? What's the problem? ----- Is she nice?"

"Well, I'm not sure if I want a serious girlfriend."

"But how will you know if you don't get to know her?"

Then he said, "I don't know if I want any real commitments."

"Why not take her out a few times and take a chance?"

"Do you think so?"

"Well, yes." I said. "Thanks for drying up, it makes a change nowadays, you're nearly always out."

It wasn't like him to seek my approval; he'd always been so independent. That's why I knew he would have a different kind of relationship with this girl. Years later I remembered this incident. On reflection, I smiled at the young son who needed to talk to his Mum before taking the first steps towards leaving the nest. At that point the last thread of the cord between us slipped away. ----- I had to let him go. He would never know that for me the next two years would feel like bereavement. Happily he made a good choice, and now has two children of his own. Will he grieve like I did when his children leave the nest? Did he learn from his parents that we are like longbows and can only be truly successful when our arrows fly to their next target?

By Chris Lammas

Sisters.

'What beach?
Down there, of course.
Which one?
Oh, it doesn't matter, any one.
Can I have a paddle?
Yes.
Shall we go down these steps?
Yes, but there are a lot.
How many?
Oh, I don't know. A lot.
I need the lavvy first.
Alright, it's over there.
Is there a queue?
No.
You won't go away?
No.'

She waited quietly on the deserted greensward.

'There, I wasn't long, was I?
No.
Can I go first?
Yes, please.
Ooh, they are steep, aren't they?
Yes.
How long will it take me to get down?
No time at all. There you go.'

----

*H*er sister was 'dead on arrival' at the bottom of the cliff, she had pushed her quite hard. Not really planned but oh my, her patience had been sorely tried.

Death by misadventure was the verdict reached after a short inquest. She, the only witness, answered questions quietly and sadly. 'Yes' her sister was of sound mind, but, 'yes', she could be a little clumsy, her sight was poor. Lacking in self confidence? 'Yes. that too.'

'We had intended having a meal here before catching the train home,' she said, 'we enjoyed all year round visits, nice to sit and watch the sea below, been coming for years. I shall miss her.'

When it was all over she intended making a new life for herself. After all, hadn't she put up with her sister's constant need for approval with her infernal questions for years and didn't she deserve to enjoy her life now that she was at last alone? Neither of them had ever married, somehow men just were never part of their lives. When their parents died, she, as the dominant one, simply took over from her mother. There was money and now she knew exactly what she wanted to do.

So, a few months after the death, she didn't care to think 'murder,' the substantial town house was sold and she returned to her favourite seaside town to live in a pleasant bungalow quite near to the sea.

She settled well after the move. She walked a lot in fine weather, enjoying the strong east coast air and preferring to stay at home when wet or windy. She relaxed, enjoying the solitude and refreshing her mind with good reading, something she had not been able to do before. She sat often on what she thought of as 'their' seat, watching the sea and daydreaming but not missing her sister. No, she was planning a holiday, a trip to Egypt. She was ready for a spot of culture.

Her neighbours were friendly. Though pleasant, she didn't encourage them and after a while they stopped inviting her in for a chat over a cup of coffee or a glass of wine. Not that she minded a glass of wine, or a chat about this and that, nothing personal, it was just that she loved the comfort of her own home. Apparently no one connected her with the unfortunate accident which had received minimal publicity just over a year ago, best to keep it that way.

So she was both surprised and annoyed when she answered a knock at the door to hear a cheerful voice say 'I heard you'd moved here, thought it was time I looked you up.' He was a middle aged man, clean and nicely dressed, but a complete stranger, as she told him in no uncertain terms.

He told her that on one of his frequent visits to the town he had seen her on the cliffs with her sister, he thought she was. 'Yes' he said, 'I saw her fall down some steps. Quite a tumble, that was.'

Her mouth was dry. She couldn't speak.

'I'll pop round tonight for a drink, we've something to talk about. Cheerio for now.' His manner was friendly.

Thoroughly shaken she returned to the sitting room, her mind whirling. Too nervous to sit she left the bungalow and walked to 'their' seat. As usual the sea calmed her. She looked around, he must have been hidden from her, probably sitting in one of the shelters on the greensward. Fool that she was to think herself unobserved. Now she must face him, listen to him. Obviously he wanted something, probably money. He could bleed her dry. Well, she had some but of one thing she was certain. He would not cause her to leave her home. After all, it wasn't too difficult to be rid of problems. Feeling calmer she walked back, ready for him.

He bounced in, full of good humour. 'No, I don't want your money, well, perhaps some of it. Need a place to live, that's all.'

She sat, rigid.

'I'll tell you. I've been living with a lady friend for years but now she has found somebody else, thrown me out and sold up. I'm paying the earth for a pokey little flat and I'm absolutely no good at living alone. Hate it. So, as I see it, it makes sense for me to move in with you. I'll have a whisky, please, and don't look so shocked. You owe me for keeping quiet.'

'You must be mad. I'm not sharing my home with you.'

A hint of something else behind the smiles. 'It's your choice. That or the place without you, I would soon find someone to share it with me. Now think about it. You're not a bad looking woman for your age. I'm clean and house trained, like gardening and I'm a good driver. We could buy a car and get about a bit, see the countryside. Give it a thought, nothing worse than a lonely old age you know. See you tomorrow.'

She tossed and turned in her bed that night, dreams in tatters but she was above all else a realist. She knew she had to accept the situation for now.

He wanted to move in straight away 'might as well start living a little' he said. She felt manipulated, as indeed she was, but strangely docile. He chose his bedroom, making it quite clear that he would also expect to be welcomed into hers. She shrugged inwardly, after all he was quite handsome and she had always wondered how it would be, she'd never been with a man. Pruney old virgins her sister had called them both.

He was friendly towards others and after a time they were accepted in the neighbourhood as a couple enjoying a late romance. She bought a car, they went on picnics, shopping trips, visited local cinemas and theatres, doing most things together since neither dared to leave the other alone for long.

Except that he liked rough weather. Delighted in walking on the cliffs in high winds and rain. Said he fought the elements. She would never join him in bad conditions but found to her surprise that she worried about him. 'Do wrap up' she would say, 'don't catch cold, you don't want another chesty cough.' Or 'Why don't you take a walking stick?' Even 'Please don't go out today, stay with me.'

In fact she realised with some pleasure that she had become very fond of him and enjoyed all aspects of their life together. She now bought herself smarter clothes for his approval and visited a hair stylist regularly, enjoying his compliments.

Towards the end of that winter severe weather took over the coastline, weather he really enjoyed and he took long walks every day, returning always to a cheerful greeting and a warm fire. On the day that he was very late back she went to look for him but saw no-one. The cliff top was deserted. She was distraught. She rang his mobile again and again but he was not answering. His wardrobe was full of the new clothes she had bought him and his toiletries were in the bathroom. She waited and hoped he would return.

When the doorbell rang she ran to answer, he had probably forgotten his key but when she opened the door there were two people waiting, a police sergeant and a woman constable.

They told her he had apparently been blown off the cliff and the fall had killed him. They had identified him from a letter in his wallet. A letter giving her name and address.

They arrested her for questioning since the letter suggested that should he meet a violent end, particularly on the cliff, she could be responsible.

'Were you out on the cliff this afternoon, ma'am?'

Crying bitter tears she nodded, 'Yes.'

By Roma Butcher.

Happy Birthday

Why have I woken?
What is that noise?
Water rushing and surging,
I'm caught in the flow.
Pulling me, pushing me;
I don't want to go.
Voices calling and urging,
excited and loud.
It's colder now-
and getting colder.
Hard steel clamps are
on my shoulder.
Ah! That's better, a warm
soft blanket.
Through eyes squeezed tight
a bright light I see.
Waaahh! Waaahh! What is that noise?
WAAAHH!! Oh Hell! - It's me!

By Patricia Barber.

157

'Til Death Us Do Part

"Soon be there, home sweet home" she cooed.

"It may be home sweet home to you" thought Charles, but to me, it's just a prison without bars. "Very soon" he thought, " I'll be retired and there'll be no work to escape to."

When Charles and Sue had married nearly forty years ago Sue had been a beautiful gentle wife but as the years had gone by she had become more and more controlling.

"Charles, don't just sit there watching your silly sports program, you know I want you to help me strip the bed and make up the spare room. You know Margaret is coming tomorrow."

Margaret was her sister and her frequent visits ensured that, for a change, the constant stream of commands were in stereo.

"Fetch my slippers from the kitchen Charles and while you're there put the kettle on."

Both of them seemed convinced that Charlie's work on the production line at Ford's was merely rest and that when he came home there they were sitting, waiting for him to start work.

But Charlie's major irritation was chauffeuring Sue, to the shops, to her sisters, a day out, whatever. Sue did not drive but she controlled Charlie's entire world from the passenger seat.

"Don't drive so fast. Don't go that way. Mind that little girl. That's not you're right of way." The commands were incessant.

Worse still these commands were to the accompaniment of loud Radio 2. Charlie hated it. When he was in the car by himself he loved the serenity of Classic FM but as soon as Sue was in the car she changed to 2 and turned up the volume and at the end of these periods of acute torture she would coo;

"Soon be there, home sweet home."

When Sue suddenly died of a massive stroke, Charles, at first felt that his world was empty but as the weeks passed he found the gentle satisfaction of peace. In the car Classic FM soothed all cares, and the prospect of retirement was a joy to be looked forward to.

The first minor irritation was the car radio. Of its own accord it would jump from Classic FM to Radio 2. Charles got it fixed but then Classic FM reception would break up a little and voices from another program could sometimes be heard. Charles began to think of getting a new car radio or perhaps even a new; more sporty car.

One misty evening, as Charlie drove home from his newly discovered snooker club, the radio reception was at it's worst. He tried re-tuning and then, as clear as if she were sitting next to him, he heard:

"Turn left here, that's it; don't drive too fast it's getting foggy. Take the road toward Cliff Way, I want to look at the sea."

Years of conditioning are impossible to resist. Charles did as he was told.

"Good it's not so foggy here, you don't need to dawdle so. That's it. Faster. Now; TURN LEFT."

As the car lurched off the cliff top Charles heard those final, fatal words:

"Soon be there, home sweet home."

By Jack Hopkins

The Spitfire

Stuart is my best friend. We are both ten years old, but Stuart is bigger and stronger. He has straight blond hair, while mine is red and curly. Nobody picks on Stuart, but everybody picks on me! --- It's on account of my hair, you see. It seems silly, but what used to be my crowning glory is now my downfall. When I was little, everyone used to say what lovely hair I had. Sometimes, when I was sitting in my pram or push-chair, ladies would come over and tousle my hair and go all gooey-eyed. Ah me, those were the days!

Since I started Junior School, I get called ginger, carrot top, and duracell. --- Some of the boys tease me, and play tricks on me in order to make me lose my temper, which isn't hard to do! I used to hate my hair, I wanted to have it all cut off, but Mum wouldn't let me. Mind you, the other kids leave me alone if Stuart is around.

We love the Summer because we get such a long, long holiday from school. It's wonderful to walk out of the gate on the last day of term with six weeks of glorious freedom stretching out in front of you. We live in the same street and we always play together. Sometimes my little brother and Stuart's sister play with us, but we like to have adventures on our own. We like riding over to the forest on our bikes to go exploring.

This last Summer we got it into our heads to go and look for the Spitfire. ------ I'll tell you how we heard about it. I usually take my Dad's stories with a pinch of salt, but there was one that caught my imagination. Mum and Dad belong to the Ramblers, and sometimes they make me and Matt (my brother) go on long boring walks. We were walking one day over at Fisher's Green near Waltham Abbey, and we went round a big lake that used to be a gravel pit. Dad told us that during the war, he saw a Spitfire and a Messerschmitt in a dog-fight. And the Spitfire was shot down, and crashed into this same gravel pit. He said it was still there, lying in twenty feet of water. Still intact he said.

So, one sunny morning, me and Stuart took our cozzies and towels, and Stuart's swimming goggles, and set off for Fisher's Green on our bikes. You have to go across the park to Enfield Lock, and along the River Lea towpath, past Waltham Abbey. We weren't sure exactly how we were going to spot the Spitfire, we just had an idea that we would swim out a little way, and dive down with the goggles on, and see what we could see.

We parked our bikes and walked around the lake. There were places where the trees and bushes grew right next to the water; it was a terrific place alright. There were lots of coves and beaches, some almost hidden in the undergrowth. To our absolute delight, near one little beach, we found a raft! It had been camouflaged with branches and tufts of grass. It was made of four oil-drums, to which planks of wood had been crudely lashed. There was also a length of wood that had been fashioned into a paddle. Stuart sent me back to fetch the bikes while he untied the raft. We felt no guilt about using it; we had every intention of returning it to it's hiding place.

We quickly changed into our cozzies, leaving our clothes and towels next to our bikes. It wasn't easy manoeuvering the raft because it was very unsteady, but we managed, and soon we were more or less at the centre of the lake.

Stuart went in first, putting on the goggles and slipping over the side. I watched him dive down, kicking hard to get some depth, and he soon disappeared from view. I just lay there, watching his bubbles, and then I saw his blond head appear as he returned to the surface. "Can't see a blindin' thing," he said.

"Could you see the bottom?" I asked. "Maybe we're in the wrong part of the lake."

"Nah," he grunted, "couldn't see the bottom, couldn't see nuthin,' just black. We'll move on a bit, and then you can have a go."

We paddled on a bit further, and with a thrill of excitement, I put the goggles on. *I* had no intention of just slipping over the side, my Dad had recently taught me to dive. In I went, head first, and the cold hit me like a watery fist. My curiosity got the better of my normal common-sense, and I continued on down. I discovered that the sunlight only penetrated down about six feet, the depths beyond were jet black.

I knew then that I had no chance of seeing *anything*, let alone my Dad's phantom Spitfire, but some demon made me dive on into the darkness. I got down to fifteen feet or so, when with a shock I felt a terrible pain. It was stomach cramp. I'd heard other people talk about it, but I'd never experienced it myself. Problem was, I was actually doubled up in the water, unable to continue swimming. In my distress, I even had difficulty in knowing which way was up.

The deep breath I had taken before diving was nearly used up, but the air in my lungs was slowly taking me towards the surface. I glimpsed faint light above. There was still some nine feet of water between me and the surface, and I couldn't hold my breath any longer. I blew the stale air out, and as a result I started to sink.

You know they say that your life flashes before your eyes just before you die? --- Well, it's true! Images appeared before me of my Mum and Dad, my sisters and my brother, my teachers at school, Stuart, all my other friends, and even the kids that used to bully me. I saw things that had happened to me years before, things that I thought I had forgotten. I remember thinking what a lot of living I had done in just ten years.

I knew that I was drowning, but I couldn't do anything about it. I started to splutter and choke as my reflexes kicked in and I instinctively tried to breathe under water. Miraculously, something gripped my hair. ------- My lovely, thick, curly *red* hair! Suddenly I was rising swiftly through the lightening water. As my head broke the surface I gulped a lungful of sweet, life-saving air, but I needed Stuart's strength to get me back on the raft.

He pulled me bodily onto the flat surface, and I lay there for what seemed like hours, coughing, spluttering, and retching the water up out of my lungs. Stuart lay there too, gasping from his exertions, and he told me that I'd been under the water for over three minutes. He had caught a glimpse of my red hair rising, and when it started to sink again, he realised that I was in trouble and leaped in to rescue me.

I wish I could explain to you how I felt, laying on that raft, looking up at the wonderful blue sky. I was shattered, but also happy, because I was still alive! -----

Thanks to Stuart *and* my red hair. A special bond was forged that day between Stuart and me, and I know that whatever becomes of us, we shall always be friends.

By Bill Davies

The Scarecrow.

Her dress torn by wind and weather
Turnip eyes watching the broken gate
Stiff wooden body with string held together
Pots and pans clink from her skinny waist.
At night when no humans are looking
She would walk, legs creaking and bent
Past shadowed trees to the brooklet
Picking flowers, inhaling their scent.
A scarecrow, a man made from sticks
To kiss, touch, none to discover
That two sentinels could be lovesick.
Daybreak lights the darkened weald
They part, shuffling back to separate fields.

By Pamela Harris.

A Close Encounter

The yellow eyes bored into mine. As the lips parted I saw fangs dripping with saliva. I was petrified, frozen with fear. The beast was so close I could hear it panting. White steam hissed from its mouth, evaporating in the freezing night air. My heart was banging, my mouth was dry, my legs started shaking. I stared into those blood-shot eyes. 'Still now! Still! Don't show your fear, stand your ground. Despite my terror, the brain was still capable of rational thought. After what seemed like hours a desperate plan occurred to me. 'Uhh muhh shhh' *stamp*. 'Uhh muhh shhh' *stamp*. I started my Maori dance. I saw a flicker of fear in the panther's eyes, then with a snarl he lowered hid head and loped submissively off. The moon was so bright it illuminated the scene as if it were day-time. After a second the beast stopped and looked back at me as if to say, "You won this time!" Then, head up, it gathered speed and raced across the field, an elegant powerful streak. I watched until it disappeared.

Trudging back down the lane, I lit my third cigarette. I soon reached the Pub garden. Wiping my clammy wet face and taking deep breaths, I walked into the welcoming warmth, noise, and light inside.

"Thought you had an early start tomorrow!"

"Forget your mobile phone again?"

"Fancy another pint?"

The friendly mocking came as my mates took in my dishevelled appearance.

"No, double scotch this time please."

Sipping my whisky, I told my tale. The next week the local rag printed this headline: *'Rugby Player encounters Black Panther!'* The article read as follows, 'Peter Black, a rugby player originally from New Zealand had a terrible shock when he was faced late at night with a black panther near Weeley Woods. Asked if he was scared Peter replied, "No, I was surprised, but not scared. I've met bigger and uglier critters on the rugby pitch." The article was accompanied by a picture of me leaning on a farm gate and pointing across the field.

My mates ribbed me for weeks. When we were in the pub they would tap me on the shoulder and snarl and growl. At rugby practice they would encircle me and howl. "Very funny," I thought. Still, it made a change from the teasing about my lack of success with the girls. I couldn't deny it; I was terrified of them. I'd stutter, mumble, and even blush. Steeling myself to ask one of them out, I was mortified when I heard myself say " Excuse me, have you got the time?"

The teasing has stopped now and at last I feel like one of the lads. You see that night, filled with dutch courage I'd asked the young waitress Stacy if I could walk her home. (In case the panther was still around you understand.) Now, thirteen months later, we are married and have a baby son, and I am one very happy Kiwi son of a gun.

I think if I ever meet that beast again I'll stand him a very large steak.

By Valerie Woollcott.

Desert Girl

Locked in her heart there is a secret place
Where sun and gleaming stars forever shine.
No fear, no grim cloud, no rain on her face
No cold, no stinging sand, no ration line.
No tanks, no shells, no screaming jets
If soldiers are there they walk without arms.
There's freedom and care and when the sun sets
No curfew, no fights, no sounds of alarm.
Lonely behind her veil she holds her dream
As she wanders the shattered, lonely streets.
She's tired and dirty, this girl of sixteen
And gunfire erupts in the desert heat.
She's gone with her dream, the girl with no name
Unaided, lost in this city of shame.

By Roma Butcher.

Reflect

The mist washed and then passed over the hull and rigging. Sometimes I could see the tops of the masts and then they were gone, ceasing to exist for minutes at a time. Silently the sails caught what wind there was, seeming to push me on a never-ending journey, regardless of weather or seas. I have nothing to do now except reflect. It was my choice to go to sea; my Emily was not best pleased, but she knew it was in my blood, bless her soul! I'm past the loneliness; resigned that I was lucky this voyage would finish, I might be reunited with her. She's gone forever now I fear, as I am.

As a watchman I am a dutiful sailor; but in this calm and foggy enclosure I must be fully vigilant. I must trust not only my eyes but also my ears. In such conditions sound travels further, though muted, as the silence is heavier. And it is now that I hear it! Sometimes it sounds like music, sometimes like the talk of dolphins or whales, or some other deep-sea creature.

Most times I'm mystified; others, like tonight, it terrifies me to the bone. As it gets closer it sounds like torture: people screaming in agony, high in tone and full of hate. The fog has split the sound so I can't be sure which direction it comes from, but I believe it is from the starboard bow. So thick is the mist that I cannot even see the bow, so I move to take up position there.

There! My instincts are right: five degrees to the starboard I can see the riding lights of a vessel, and she's heading west for the Indies. A breeze has parted the fog's wall and I can tell she'll pass only a chain's distance. No matter, I am the larger, and she will have to heave to if the wind should push her too close. Ah, what a beauty! Her hull is smooth and white; her two masts abrim with sail, making the most of the gentle south-westerly breeze. How sleek! She must be reaching four knots at least. I shout my warnings but they pay no heed; then in an instant the noise has stopped as if cut by a knife, and it is silence except for the sound of her rigging, the wash of the sea, and the sigh of the wind. At last I see figures on her foredeck: six I count, at least two of them females, no less.

They are close and have sight of us. They are pointing and staring as I shout "Ahoy there" and wave; but that is all they do: point and stare, just like all the others. Their faces are young and fresh; so close that I can see every detail and I wave and shout but they can't see me: just as I can't see my crew-mates, but I know they're here. I watch the sleek beauty disappear behind God's curtains, and I wonder if I'm in the same place as Emily, or will she too be unseen for eternity.

I take up my watch station again, and it's just as before: me and the Marie Celeste and my unseen crew-mates for ever reflecting, though I doubt we cast no shadow nor reflection.

By Simon Butcher

Victoria

Dear sweet sugar plum, luscious, so tasty.

I wish you were mine to have and savour

But you are too high to reach on the tree.

Please bend your bough, let me taste your flavour.

While you're firm of flesh you plumsious beauty,

Let go your hold, I am here to catch you.

While you're sweet and young and oh so fruity

Drop now, sweet plum before birds attack you.

A waiting maggot may infest your heart

Or wasps may dig a hole within your flesh.

Your rosy skin says you are sweet not tart.

Oh! drop, sweet plum, while you are at your best

But if you cling, dear plum and drop not soon

Remember, sweet plums are tomorrow's prune.

By Jack Hopkins

The Armchair

Anne smoothed the cold soft duvet that the case had crumpled. She stood back to check everything was back in place. She walked slowly and thoughtfully down the stairs. This morning had been quite a shock Her daughter had stayed for the weekend. It had been good to have her there, cooking her favourite food and watching the television together. Since she had been to University she had met Nigel. Of course Anne had not met him, but Jenny was so keen, and had decided to move in with him.

They had been packing her suitcase when Anne had said, "My only hope is that he's as good a partner as your father was to me." (She had lost her husband Tom seven months ago.)

Her daughter had stopped, stood up, and stared at her. She took a deep breath and blurted, "If Nigel was anything like Dad I'd run a mile. You always say how much he understood you, put up with your bad nerves, but don't you realise it was you trying to keep him totally happy that caused them. Dad was a total control freak."

Anne burst into tears. "How can you speak like that about the dear man?"

Jenny moved close to hold her mother, but added, "I'm sorry Mum, but I've held onto my thoughts for a long long time."

They had left the packing and made tea. It appeared that now Jenny had started, she had to go on. "Can you imagine how Dad would have reacted once he knew about Nigel? Dad's third degree would have scared the hell out of him. I couldn't have a proper life until I left home. Dad would have done his best to control the two of us as much as he did you."

"But Jenny, he was so good. He wanted to keep us safe. You always knew he would give you anything you wanted. He was such a generous man. I always had the best. Your Dad made sure I always looked good."

"Mum, when was the last time you chose something for yourself? Or made any decision in this family? Dad did it all. You never had any money of your own, and when you came back from the shops, you even gave him the change that was left over, just like a child. *He* ruled the roost."

After Jenny left, she had time to reflect. Anne looked at the now empty armchair that Tom had always commandeered. She had never sat in it. It had been his throne and now, a shrine.

She knew her daughter was right. Since she had left her job to marry for security, she had learned to be childlike, helpless and dependent. Now she was alone. She walked deliberately over to that chair and sat down. She knew now why Tom had liked it so much. It felt good.

By Chris Lammas

Over Fifties Aerobics Class

Wednesday dawned with the lifting of the eyelids, the alerting of the mind to another day's events ahead. The realisation that the afternoon heralded the Wednesday's Over Fifties Exercise class. One hour of sheer torture. The chosen few assemble at the top of the stairs at the studio, looking down at the instruments of sheer pain, heaven knows what all the apparatus is for. There they stand, grey, dark, and looming. Their promise of perfection is hard to see amongst their iron and steel-clad armour.

A few hardy souls are already pounding their hearts and socks off, treading away imaginary miles. Patches of moisture wetting brows and Lycra. Brightly coloured, tight fitting clothing. I hope they get to their destination. It looks impressive.

We the middle-aged brigade make our way downstairs, past more machines, which I swear smile as we pass, ready to pounce, their jaws already snaring a couple of victims, like rabbits in the glare of headlights, unable to escape. Entrapped by arms and legs, contorting bodies into unnatural shapes. I wonder if they realise that the human frame does not really want to do this, it would rather be slumped in an armchair with a cup of sweet tea and buttered scone to hand.

Reaching the appropriate room, which feels very cold, no window to detract the commitment of mind and body of better things to do. One wall, completely mirrored, faces the victims. We try not to look at distended bellies and flabby arms.

We chat with our Instructor, with her perfect figure, and pretty young face, which we all once had, but many years of babies, work, and HRT have changed us into what we are now. We want to restore our pristine beauty!

Instructor dons her microphone or whatever it is to her waist, tunes in the very loud tape machine, as we, the short, tall, fat, thin, clad in our tee-shirts, track suits or whatever, reluctantly form into some sort of order to begin our quest. We do the basic warm-up, bodies warming up and swaying to the constant unrelenting beat of music and movement.

Looking at the clock, surely it is more than five minutes since we began! Only fifty-five to go. Back and forth we move as one, out of step, out of breath, faces reddening with exertion. Does not 'She who must be obeyed' realise that I am not the same shape as her? That bellies get in the way of flaying arms? That busts are bigger and floppier than her muscle toned tightness? That we are heavier in frame than this delicate sugarplum fairy in front of us!

I'll have a drink; this takes a few seconds respite from the unending pace. Another look at the clock, oh good, it's a quarter past, only forty-five minutes to go. Hearts pound, legs stretch, joints and muscles long unused scream with pain. Can she not hear them? Please slow down, must not let the others down by stopping. On and on, stretch, breathe, feeling hot, cannot co-ordinate my parts.

At last we wind down, heart, bones, everything sighs with relief as we end the session.

Upstairs we go to the normal world, laugh at ourselves for our mistakes. Despite all the weariness, tell each other that we will meet the next week. Go home with smiles on our faces and in our hearts, ready to gird ourselves for next week's session.

By Pamela Harris

The Giraffalapotamus

I am a Giraffalapotamus
We don't make much noise or a lotoffuss
We live in the city
And it's oh such a pity
That breeding is largely unknown to us

I have a large tumical belly
And spend all day watching the telly
My neck is quite long
And I think it's all wrong
That I have to exist on pink jelly

I hate all the Ligers and Tigons
They won't let our quarrels be bygones
They chase us all day
And they won't go away
Causing hefflants to suffer trunkations

Us Animules don't like to grumble
Instead of complaining we mumble
When the going gets tough
We stutter and bluff
And go back to live in the Jumble

By Bill Davies

A Busy Person.

*W*aking with the alarm it was but a minute before the usual feeling of emptiness came with consciousness, as it does every morning. This, together with the fear of the long day stretching ahead began testing my willpower and the urge to simply turn over and sleep the day away. I must not do that. Moving quickly into the bathroom preparations for a busy day began, I have to leave the house in one hour.

In my briefcase I have all that I need for the day, a yellow legal pad, pens, pencils and my diary. A few printed documents and a mobile telephone.

I am on my way to the local airport and today will be meeting the 9.52 a.m. from Paris, normally only half full with men and women wearing sharp business suits and looking as I am now, smart, efficient, stressed.

Arrivals is pleasantly full and after checking the board I choose a seat where I can easily watch all the comings and goings. Assuming a work weary expression I open my briefcase, make a note in the diary, glance again at the board and, removing a closely printed document check my watch before carefully reading the instructions for a rather simple fish pie, pausing now and then to stare at nothing, obviously deep in thought and making a few notes in my legal pad. With a deep sigh and clear irritation I circle one such note, frowning and tapping the paper with my pen. An arguable point? No, I'm out of eggs.

By now the plane has landed and I stand to watch passengers busily striding through, some being met, some but not all with a seemingly strong sense of purpose. Then the last one is past and I am still standing, looking perplexed. After a while I shrug, check the board again, look at my watch and frowning, return to my seat. Taking out my mobile I speak angrily for a few minutes to a colleague known as J.J.

Of course the non arrival of my contact means a long wait for the next flight in from Paris and that means buying a daily newspaper, the Financial Times naturally. Settled in my seat once more I carefully peruse the stocks and shares, again making notes. Lots of foot tapping and ominous signs of frustration. Can I afford to waste this time? Is anyone looking? Does anyone care?

No. I take out another printed sheet. This one tells me how through near starvation I can lose ten pounds in one week and look wonderful. Riveting stuff. I put a large cross though this page and consider my next move.

The 'plane is due in at 3.05 p.m., having so obviously been bored silly for a while it is time to have a gin and tonic, sitting confidently at the bar. No lunch, we career women are supposed to be thin aren't we? Perhaps another one just to kill time.

A lengthy visit to the Ladies Room to check my already immaculate hair and make-up, a stroll around the book shop and I return to await the 'plane's arrival, only another hour.

With a frosty glance around the room I choose another seat and text a message to my home number, reminding me that not only am I out of eggs but tea-bags should also go on the list. And tonic water. I make more notes, read an article on bunions, check the board a hundred times and finally, just before the 'plane is due, relax.

Again, all the passengers stream past, intent and purposeful. After a pained look around I leave, speaking angrily on my silent mobile to the unfortunate J.J.

Smart shoes are hurting my feet so I take a taxi the few miles home. Expenses, after all.

I clear the answer phone, note eggs, teabags and tonic water on the kitchen board then sit with tea in my extremely comfortable lounge with it's original paintings and fine ornaments, It has been a long day and I am quite tired but before I make supper there is tomorrow to plan. Perhaps I'll go to Stansted, it will mean driving but that's alright. I might even get the morning flight to Schipol and spend the day there. I can afford it after all, my redundancy settlement had been very generous indeed and I have only myself to please. Best to keep busy.

By Roma Butcher.

The Party

I glance at my watch; soon the family will arrive. Just got time for a lick of nail polish and to fix diamante clips to my new dress.

Ross toddles into the bedroom, his starfish hands opening and closing, arms outstretched. "Cuddles pleath" he lisps.

"Sorry darling, I'll smudge my nails." I blow a raspberry on the back of his warm pink neck; chuckling, he puts his head on my knee for more. I inhale his sweet innocence, the fragrance of baby soap and talc.

As the doorbell rings Ross lurches off to greet more besotted admirers. I hear voices and laughter downstairs, the party has started. I love New Year's Eve.

This year it's our turn to be host to our large family. How very different the mood will be this year compared to last. Reflecting on the last twelve months I feel that I have journeyed to a dark dangerous place, stumbling blindly home to warmth and safety.

I can hear Ross bumping down the stairs on his bottom, trying to count, "one, two, three." This morning, friends had helped me to prepare for the party. As they worked they were making New Year resolutions.

I smile as I remembered pretty plump Abbi stuffing the vol-au-vents dejectedly, saying, "I must lose weight!" She turned to me angrily. "Not all of us can eat everything in sight and stay stick-thin!" Tess was saying that she was going to have to give up her favourite black tipple as it made her hyper. I do not have that problem, I hate the stuff. Smoking does not appeal either, it's horrid, too smelly, besides, I can't afford it.

I suppose I should give up swearing. My parents have been very strict, I never hear them utter profanities. Some of my friends say terrible words, I think it makes them sound common. And yet, at the same time, I have a yen to be a ladette.

Fern was going to give up men *again*. She had been disgusted when two admirers had brawled in the street over her, rolling in the gutter, filthy and bloody, like animals. As she related this piece of drama from her action-packed life she was painstakingly shaping tomatoes into water lilies. She didn't see the catty gestures behind her back. We had all agreed years before that she was stunning, so it was no wonder that men dropped like flies around her.

Freya was our shy, quiet little bookworm. She blushed as she said quietly, "I have a passion for baked beans on toast, it must be on granary bread with real butter. Every time I go to the library cinema or theatre, I get terrible wind and have to pretend to cough or sneeze. It sounds like a trumpet and it is *soooooo* embarrassing, so no more beans. That's mine"

As I finish dressing, I wonder what my resolution should be. Pulling my sparkly party shoes from my wardrobe my hand touches a box. A frisson of excitement runs through me, my new ice skates! Bright red soft leather, blades shining, catching the light. My best Christmas present ever; they came with a year's pass to the local rink, it lays nestling in the tissue paper.

My resolution is to practise and practise, and to enter for the Winter Olympics. Then afterwards I can join a top skating show, as the leading lady of course! I can do it, I know I can!

I run my hand over the soft stubble of my scalp. The hair is growing fast, but I still look like a hedgehog. My treatment has finished, and the doctors are pleased. It was strange how in the beginning people stopped speaking when I came into a room, then started chatting loudly. Only Ross acted normally. Once I heard Granddad say to my Mum, "The lass has got a hard road to travel, but she's a fighter, and youth is on her side."

I pull on my long glossy wig, from hedgehog to Fern in one easy go! Swishing the hair from side to side, coyly playing with a strand, but no matter how hard I try to impersonate my friend, somehow the effect is not the same. Never mind! We cannot all have beauty and talent! ------- Maybe if I try lowering my eyelashes?

This time next year I shall be skating my way to fame and fortune. I laugh as I slick on my lip-gloss. And all before my thirteenth birthday!

By Valerie Woollcott

Free Spirit.

I do not crave sun, sand or sea
But places where my spirit is free
To wander valleys, past streams that flow
Over stones, watching sunsets glow.
I see peaceful tall trees that shade
Fresh peaty soil, clad boots that tread
Pathways and lanes; twigs touch my head
Sheep on hills, cows ambling homeward
Freedom to be able to roam
Bare slopes where chasing shadows skim
Through gaps of ancient woodland dim.
Giant oaks waving branches dark
To soft green lichen clinging to bark.
Wrap my old limbs with ivy twine
Combine with nature, this my shrine.

By Pamela Harris.

Cliff-Hanger

"*A* trumpet shall sound," Maestro looks at me and I stand up. Flick the valves, lick my lips and I'm ready, I hope.

I should not be here really but Fulford rang this morning to say that he had cut his lip shaving and would not be able to play. It's a poor excuse really. All the orchestra knows that the poor little wimp gets regularly beaten by his dominating wife and that it was only a matter of time before she fetched him one round the lip. But, what's a fat lip for Fulford is good luck for me. I'm a good trumpet player but I was Silver Band trained rather than a product of academic musical training like the rest and I feel inferior.

Anyway! Maestro called me in this morning and asked me if I was able to play trumpet solo at tonight's performance so here I am, Westminster Abbey, top row standing. Maestro said

I should stand so that the audience should experience what was in effect a duet of solo tenor and Trumpet.

He is a super tenor, tubby with a little moustache; I think the soprano has got the hots for him she's looking up at him as though she wants to eat him. Of course I told Maestro that I was up for it. What I did not tell him was the dream I had last night. How I was standing alone on stage, with a large crowd looking on. I raise my trumpet to my lips, hit the note and, nothing. Well not exactly nothing, no sound just large bubble from the bell. The audience is laughing. I blow again and a huge bubble appears. My trousers seem to be slipping down and the audience is throwing rotten fruit.

Angela is sitting in the front row. She is sneering. I just pray that my dream is not prophetic. My pulse is raising, Maestro looks at me ready to give me the beat.

Angela is sitting just below me. She plays first cello. I have never met anyone like her. She is beautiful, educated, intelligent and she holds that Cello between her knees like she was making love to it. I hope that my performance this evening will impress her and maybe we would make music together without the aid of any musical instruments. I can imagine Angela, holding me like the Cello with her hands clutched round my back. A man could die happy between Angela's knees.

But, what if my dream becomes reality. I remember going to a concert where a flutist was giving a recital and instead of a pure first note he got a gob of spit on the mouthpiece and all he got was a gurgle. I give him full marks for bravery. He stopped, got out a handkerchief, wiped the mouthpiece and started again but I blushed for him all the way through the recital. My God! It could happen to me.

Angela looks up. She is smiling at me. Is that a promise of pleasures to come? Sweat is pouring down both sides of my face. I taste the salt on my lips. Have I time to wipe my mouth? No, now is the moment.

It is the Easter concert at Westminster Abbey, the Messiah and I John Brown, brass band player from Pickerskill, new member of the BBC Symphony Orchestra am about to make an absolute idiot of myself.

Maestro twitches a nonchalant baton at me and I hit the note. It is as though my horn is made of pure gold. The liquid notes caress every nook and cranny of the Abbey.

"And the dead shall be raised."

My bit again, I hope Angela finds my golden horn irresistible.

By Jack Hopkins

Rock Chick

I want to be a Hell's Angel Rock Chick
Dyed orange hair, safety pins and attitude
Coal black eyes, bright red lipstick

Swirling chains standing in front of the heartsick
A sex symbol performing to multitudes
I want to be a Hell's Angel Rock Chick

With buckling legs this elderly phobic
Drink and drugs transport me to ineptitude
Coal black eyes, bright red lipstick

Electric guitars,bass throbbing, drumsticks,
My age not considered easy platitude
I want to be a Hell's Angel Rock Chick

Pounding beat sends brain-dead dancers orgasmic
Never to regret nights of my future solitude
Coal black eyes, bright red lipstick

I'm a leftover flower power beatnik
Get it out of my system before pending quietitude
I'm going to be a Hell's Angel Rock Chick
Coal black eyes, bright red lipstick.

By Pamela Harris (Age 74)

Mrs Jeffers House Is A Shambles

It used to be such a joy to be there, tucked away on the top shelf behind the shop door. I could sit and watch as people and cars went by, up and down the street towards the underground tube station. For four years I sat in that corner at Randolph and Baker Antiques Ltd. It was a wonderful life really. No-one seemed to notice me or show any interest in me except Mr. Randolph --- or Randy as he was called by his friends. He dusted me every two days. In fact he dusted all of us, but to me it was always a special occasion as he gently lifted me and rearranged my position. Randy was thorough and neat, with strong, gentle hands. His voice was gentle and soft too as he told me how precious and priceless I was; it did not matter that no-one else noticed me. I glowed with pride as I sat proudly, enthroned high above all others, on the top shelf.

But all this changed when Mr. Baker, Randy's partner, quietly passed on last month. He had not been into the shop for some time and things had been quieter than usual. Mrs. Baker, the widow, said she couldn't manage the shop and, as Randy hadn't the money to buy out her share of the business, the shop must close and everything must go. Each day had been a nightmare as we waited to be disposed of, and each evening the fear grew that those of us who remained would be cast away; dumped in that horrible skip sitting on the road outside. I was desperate to find a new home. Most of the others had already been taken. I overheard Mrs. Baker say I was clumsy and no-one will have me, so, I will have to be thrown away. I was terrified as the last day arrived. Then the heavy door swung open and there stood Mrs. Jeffers – not very tall and dressed in a black lace embroidered shawl over a knee length red satin skirt. She was coming my way and my heart quickened with excitement. I did not want to leave but I must.

We had quite a long journey and I had time to ponder and wonder about my new home. At last we were there at Jeffers Cottage. I held my breath as I was brought out and took my first glance around my new home.

Nothing in my life could ever have prepared me for what I saw. The place was a shambles! At the far end of the room was an old rocking chair, with a large grandfather clock next to it and, a small round table holding a large vase with Chinese painting on it in many different colours and shapes. There was also a picture frame with a photograph of two people who could only be Mr. and Mrs. Jeffers. On one side of the room was a brown and white rug, half rolled up; supporting several garden ornaments, some squirrels, two ducks, and what looked like a small water fountain. Three mustard coloured cats sat motionless on a tall chair, and on the floor beside them a plastic bowl full of old magazines and used empty envelopes. A stuffed rabbit with piercing eyes sat on one end of a couch on the other side of the room. They all looked so lifeless and full of dust.

'Where will I fit?' I shivered.

I am not very large but I do need space to show myself to advantage. There seemed to be no room for me in all this muddle. Then, as I was carried forward by Mrs Jeffers, I spotted an old glass- fronted cabinet in the darkest part of the room.

'Oh no! She wouldn't!' I thought, - but she did. Just as I was just about to make my stand a loud squawk filled the room and, to my horror, I saw the biggest eye I have ever seen. It was fixed on me and belonged to a parrot in a green and black wooden cage.

'Hi Ziggy, my girl!' called Mrs Jeffers. 'Look! I have brought you a new friend '.

My heart sank as she began to wind me up. I hate being wound up, it's no fun and especially here in Mrs. Jeffers shambles of a house, with Ziggy looking on. I could feel her eyes following me across the room as I crashed, bumped stumbled and rolled my way across and under the rocking chair, bumped into the fireplace and finally stuck myself behind the rug. Ziggy squawked and flapped her wings in glee, and danced around her cage.

'Oh, how I wish I could die! This is no life for a precious, priceless toy teapot on wheels'.

By Albertha Braithwaite.

Falling In Love.

Look away, look away, don't let him see

The excitement that holds you so still.

If it's not a lover you want to be

Don't let your heart know this thrill.

Don't look so deeply into his eyes

Don't see that challenging blue.

Don't think of warm sand and tropical skies

Don't think of this man holding you.

But the world is still, there's scarcely a sound

And the world is only for two.

And love is something you may have found

With this man who is looking at you.

By Roma Butcher.

Perennial

Dear Vicar,

Thank you for visiting me today. You need comfort when recently bereaved. It's a lonely time. Please feel free to call again.
Rose Waters

Dear Rose Waters,

I also enjoyed our chat, and your company. I make a point of comforting the bereaved to offer solace in times of sadness. I will call on Monday.
Lionel Baxter

Dear Lionel,

I hope you do not object to me calling you by your first name. I feel we have a close bond since you now call so often.
Rose

Dear Rose,

You are a kind woman; you make homemade cakes and tea to perfection. You did not object to my parting hug. As it was dark I do not think we were seen. See you tomorrow.
Love, Lionel

Dear Lionel,

You are such a naughty man, can't keep your hands to yourself, can you? I look forward to seeing more of you. Aren't I wicked!

Your love magnet, Rose

Darling Rose,

I will meet you in the Red Lion for a pre drink at five p.m. I've booked us a hotel room in town. We must be careful sweetie, my wife would not approve.

Can't wait, Lionel.

Dearest Lionel,

Can't wait to be alone with you, to abandon myself to your love. I'll pay all expenses.

From your darling Rose.

My Beautiful,

Our time together was beyond belief. You really are a firecracker.

Yours forever, Lionel.

Lionel my love

I have booked us in for another weekend. Hope you can get away easily.

Your darling Rose xxxxxx

Rose,

Can't manage to get away. I have notification of another bereavement at the other end of the village.

Lionel

By Pamela Harris

A Day In The Life Of Nelson

I have been up this column since eighteen forty-four, standing upright in all types of unrelenting weather, gales, rain, sun, and freezing cold. I have been photographed, stared at, and annoyed. I am just about fed up with it. Having to endure noisy protests, demonstrations and parties that always take place in the square below me.

I never wanted to be famous or be recognised for a specific part of London. The pigeons are a pest, perching on my hat and messing everywhere. In one of my quieter moments I worked out that if a bird pooed from my hat rim, it would obtain a speed of twenty-five miles per hour before landing. These birds have ruined my uniform; it's now tatty and torn. Below me are city gentlemen going to work, smart, in suits and natty hats. I want to be like them, I would like the public to see a new me.

Keeping clean is difficult; apart from a yearly wash with a power hose via the Council I rely on rain mostly. Which is rather irritating when I see four sparkling clean fountains within reach. If those lions sitting on each corner were to lose their responsibilities, maybe take a walk down the road to Buckingham Palace, or even Regents Park Zoo, then in the night I could slide down and take a shower.

I pass the time in various ways, favourite being collecting bus and car numbers. I have thousands in the notebook, which I keep in my breast pocket. I have to keep my good arm on it in case the wind whisks it away.

If I could turn around to see another part of London, my one good eye would appreciate it.

I like fog, then no one can see me and I can't see them. Then I can relax a little. Being on display all day every day is daunting. Recently they put spotlights on me so I can be seen at night. Another thing that gets up my bronze nose is photographers; flashing light bulbs make me blink. My image must be in every drawer in the whole world.

It's no fun being an icon. So, when you see me again doing my bit for England, give me a wave.

By Pamela Harris

Second Chance

Once upon a time, a young man named Arthur decided that the simple life in Happy Ever Aftia was not for him. He intended to be different. He wanted to be a Somebody and so he went to away to study, to learn a profession. Now, five years later, on the door of his pretty, red tiled roofed cottage, was a brass plaque that announced:

Arthur Grunge
Divorce Lawyer.

Each day Arthur polished the plaque and waited. Each day he examined his appointment book and each evening he turned the page to another blank sheet.

Princess Cindy looked out from the topmost castle turret. She could hear the merry village sounds but her spirits stayed low. For one thing, her feet hurt. There were 403 stone steps to climb to reach this peaceful room but she needed the peace, she needed time to think.

The sad Princess looked down at the village below. She could trace all the streets, all the shops. There was the sweetshop that sold such delicious everlasting bulls eyes there, the health and beauty salon run by her stepsisters, Hermione and Petal and there, knitting in her garden, content in her retirement, she could see her Fairy Godmother. As usual, a crowd of villagers, having seen the golden haired princess were cheering and clapping. How they loved their beautiful Princess Cindy! One has to smile and wave back, she thought but her mind kept straying to the little house on which she had seen the plaque which read: "Arthur Grunge, Divorce Lawyer."

The castle drawbridge crashed and two horsemen rode out. Cindy recognised them. It was her husband, Princy with Dandini, his constant companion.

Cindy had a busy afternoon. The Marketing Manager of the "Glass Shoe Co. (By Appt.) was showing the proposed new designs for the "Princess Line."

"Buttons, do you think anyone will want to buy these designs? They all seem so contented wearing clogs."

"Cinders, you just rely on me. I know what I'm doing. As long as you are seen wearing the designs we get all the publicity we need and we make a pile of gold selling clogs with the same designer label."

"If you say so dear Buttons. If you're sure it's legal. One must think of the foot health of all those dear villagers."

"Sure, sure, Princess, just sign here. Ta. I was chatting to your Dad this morning, he says your stepmum's gone to the Magic kingdom for a mid-week break. I think he's pleased to get the break himself."

"Perhaps one should go and visit him. Maybe he's lonely."

"Shouldn't think so Cinders, when I saw him he had all the company he could handle or, should I say, he was handling all the company he could manage. Know what I mean?" Buttons left, leaving the princess staring gloomily at one's feet.

Cindy retired early to bed that evening and it was not until much later that she was disturbed by the returning Princy.

"I'm sorry old thing, for being so late," he said, kissing her foot peeping below the duvet, "Dandy and I have been having so much fun that I did not realise how late it was."Cindy pulled back her foot under the duvet and pretended to sleep. That's it! she thought, Tomorrow morning I'm off to see Grunge!

It was never easy for the Princess to leave the castle without the waiting photographers recording the event but she had learnt that, if she stuck to a routine they soon learnt that following her would not produce more pictures than they already had. Cindy tripped across the drawbridge in her figure-hugging tracksuit and trainers, jumped into her mini-pumpkin and with a cheery smile to the photographers, zoomed away.

She did not stop at her stepsisters' gym but taking a round about route, arrived outside the lawyer's house. Disguised in dark glasses and a headscarf, she hurried to the door.

Arthur Grunge was feeling disheartened. Two years of blank diary. Two years of no work. Rat Tat what was that! Somebody at the door! For some moments he could not think what to do. This had never happened before. There was somebody at his door!

When Arthur had collected his wits enough to open the door he was surprised to see a slender, track suited lady wearing enormous sunglasses. He recognised her immediately but, panic! should he bow or curtsey? Before his mind could resolve the question she had swept by him into the hall.

"You've got to help me Mr Grunge. I am in desperate trouble." Tears rolled from beneath her dark glasses.Grunge struggled to regain his composure.

"Do you have an appointment?" he asked, scanning the pages of his diary.

"No, no, but you've got to help me. Can't you fit me in? I don't mind waiting."

Grunge looked serious. "Hmm, I think I could squeeze you in. Let's just take down a few particulars and we will see what we can do to be of assistance. Your name is?"

"Princess Cindy. I mean, Her Royal Highness The Princess Cinderella of Happy Ever Aftia."

Grunge felt his heart pounding and his palms sweating as he looked at the vision now sitting on the other side of his desk. The first person to ever sit in that chair is Princess Cindy, he thought. This is the big time!

It was not long before the Princess was pouring out her tale of woe. "Out every day with that Dandini. All he wants to do is to dress up in those stupid clothes and go to Balls. Do you know, I found him and that slug Dandini, in my bedroom wearing my best tights! They were dancing around the room slapping themselves on the thigh. He never helps me with the business. He's just off every day with that mincing, perfumed peacock Dandini. D'you know, his mother was a fairy." Cindy paused to dab her eyes.

Grunge hesitated. This was a difficult question. "Does he…. in bed? Does he er, how shall I put this? Does he perform his ah, princely duties?" Grunge felt his face flushing with embarrassment.

"Does He Perform His Princely Duties! No he does not! He slobbers all over my feet and that's it."

"That's it?" murmured Grunge. "Nothing else?"

"He's got a foot fetish. All he wants to do is kiss my feet. He doesn't think about My needs, My feelings, do you know he won't let me wear comfortable shoes! I have to wear too tight, too hard *bloody glass slippers!*" Her voice diminished from a roar to a wail of despair. "I can't bloody walk. I'm getting bunions and I Have to wear bloody glass slippers."

When all the sobbing was spent and all the notes taken Grunge showed her to the door promising to give the matter urgent priority.

Over the next few weeks Grunge wrote several letters, assuring her that all processes were in hand. There were three more interviews at which Cindy sobbed and Grunge took copious notes. Wonderful! thought Grunge. This is how the money rolls in!

To Cindy those few weeks seemed forever. On most days she visited her stepsisters, Hermione and Petal, at the health salon, not because she had any particular affection for them but because it gave her the excuse to wear tracksuits and divinely comfortable trainers. The resident chiropodist advised her that the glass slippers would cause untold problems in later life. She could not tell anyone that she was taking steps to eliminate the problem. At times, she felt envious of her ex ugly sisters. When Cinderella had become Princess Cindy and all were expected to live happily ever after, her Fairy Godmother, with a wave of her wand, had removed most of their disfiguring features. They were not beauties. Fairy Godmothers work magic, not miracles. They looked their best with the light behind them. Grunge sent her another letter suggesting that she made an urgent appointment as matters had reached crisis point.

"It seems, ah, Cindy, that we have hit a major problem. I have drawn up pleas to the courts, listing grounds of unreasonable behaviour and demanding a huge cash settlement but," He paused, shuffling his papers. "But we do not have a court to whom we can apply. I have discovered that Happy Ever Aftia does not have one. There are neither criminal nor civil courts. I have searched every record," said Grunge, gesturing at the shelves of heavy books which lined the walls. "Nothing. I can do no more."

Grunge wondered if now was the time to raise the subject of his bill. Cindy's sobs seemed to indicate that it might be better to send the huge bill to her by post. At last he managed to persuade her to leave but only by promising to continue searching for a way out of her problem.

On Saturday Grunge decided to take the day off. He felt that he deserved the rest and was walking by a stream enjoying the peace. He realised how noisy the village was every day with the continual clatter of clogs on the cobbles and the incessant trivia of the villagers' happy chatter. The only other person in view was an old lady walking her aged dog.

"Good day, young man," she quavered. It was the Fairy Godmother (By Appt.)

Arthur made all the appropriate noises about what a lovely day it was and what a wonderfully intelligent little dog and turning to go, put his foot firmly into a deposit left by that dear intelligent dog! As he struggled to wipe his shoe clean he thought, it's all that stupid old woman's fault! And then he had a brilliant idea.

At home he sat at his desk. This would require careful thought. It would affect so many people. Yes. It would work. He would go for an annulment on the grounds of non-consummation of marriage and he would appeal to the Fairy Godmother (By Appt.) She started it so she must finish it.

Arthur Grunge, Divorce Lawyer, sent a letter to the FGM (By Appt.) asking if she would call to see him at a mutually convenient time.

"So you see Godma'am, it is all your fault. Your magic has caused my client, The Princess Cinderella, grievous harm and she will look to you for restitution."

"But what can I do? I'm retired. I can't fly now you know. I get dizzy. It's the vertigo." She paused and thought. If she could undo her "Good Deed" it would mean turning the clock back. In the process she too would turn back. She too would be younger. She would be rid of this nagging rheumatism.

"I'll do it," she said, rummaging through her bag. Shedding wool and knitting needles, she exhumed a battered wand and clearing her throat, she warbled,

"Because of Cindy's tears,
let us annul these past sad years."

The wand twinkled and Happy Ever Aftia swirled in a maelstrom of collapsing time...............

Cinderella sat beside the dying fire, toasting her pretty toes as she listened to the sounds of her Father, Stepmother, Hermione and Petal, leaving for the Ball. Buttons was making the cocoa and she was looking forward to a quiet evening when she and Buttons could dream their future.

The dark corner of the room lightened as the Hairy Godmother appeared. Cinderella sighed, what a time to have visitors! Just when she was having some peace and quiet.

"I am your Fairy Godmother. Tell me child, how can I help you to be happy?"

Cinderella took a deep breath. Chances like this come only once or maybe twice in a lifetime.

"Oh, Fairy Godmother, Buttons and I love each other. We want to get married."

"But how will you live, my child?"

Cinderella pulled from her apron pocket the cash flow and expenditure charts that she and Buttons had imagined.

"We have this dream of setting up a double glazing company, but we don't have the cash to start."

"Fetch me a pumpkin and six white rats," said the FGM. She did not know why but she vaguely remembered that that was the proper way to proceed. It was not easy but by using a doubtful rhyme she was able to compose a spelling charm in which Cinders was rhymed with winders.

The magic wand twinkled and the pumpkin became a factory on a brown field site and the six white rats became six of the finest double-glazing salesmen.

At the Ball Prince Charming was explaining to Dandini that people were beginning to talk.

"I really do not know was all the fuss is about, Dandy old chap but we need wives and as he spoke, Hermione and Petal made their entrance.

"I say Princy, look at those two old boots!"

It could not be said that it was love a first sight but the Prince knew that he could include an old boot in his foot fetish.

Arthur Grunge is back at University studying Sociology. He intends to become a social worker.

And they all lived happily ever after.

The End

By Jack Hopkins

Jake's Ride

It was cramped in the lift. Otis said twelve people. --- I made fourteen. The guy nearest the buttons asked which floor and I said "seventeen" I heard the broad behind me mutter "shit!" Was I cramping her style -- or had I farted? I don't give a diddly squat. The doors seemed keen to close - either side competing to get to the middle first. We jerked skyward.

It was just before nine in the morning and the suits were heading for their cells. Eight hours a day to pay off their credit, twenty-four to worry why the f*** you got it in the first place.

No such problems for me! I'm at the top. I'm forty-eight and I'm a God. I bet every one of these saps owes me. I am their God --- *your God,* the face behind the forms you sign when you want a new fridge, or hi-fi, or car, anything you want as long as it's better than your neighbours. But hey! No worries!

Pretty soon your neighbour will be in wanting a new form. ---
Mine of course, --- making sure you've soon got to come back
for another one. And of course you can have it but you gotta
go back to jail to pay for it. Saps. -- All of you!

Me -- I deserve the best. I make it all possible for you. I
make sure you have to work your pleasures away, 24/7. Nothing
but the best for me. I'd seen the ad in the top people's magazine
"We make sure you get the reward you deserve. --- Ultimate
Destinations and Sons 17th floor McCarthy Building." So
here I was. I know there will be a payoff for this but I reckon
a South Sea island with all the trimmings is what I deserve so
that's what I'm gonna pay for.

The lift was impersonating its Coney Island cousin, trying
to heave the coffee out of my stomach like a fairground ride.
Different odours with bodies were getting off, nobody was
getting on. It seemed every floor lay in wait for someone. There
were smokers and chewers, nancies and bimbos, overwashed
and untouched. I could smell them all. But they had one
stench in common ----- money. My money. They didn't know
it but they all worked for me.

We made it to the sixteenth and sure enough Miss Shitty
got off. The doors did a head to head and we shook free again
only this time just me and one other guy, another suit, only
older than the others, maybe my age. Like me he was leaning
against the wall rail, protecting his coffee. I smiled a "Hi!" and
got the same back.

It seemed a long way between floors and I moved over to the buttons to check. There was no seventeen! They stopped at sixteen! I shot my eyes up to the digital counter. -- It still said sixteen but we were headed upward. I pushed the 'Stop' button, the 'Open Doors' the 'Emergency' -- every f***ing button I could ------ but still we climbed. I panicked. --- Shit, I'm a moneylender, I don't panic!

I turned to the guy behind. Funny, he was still smiling.

"Welcome to Ultimate Destinations Jake. All the way to the top was it?"

By Simon Butcher

Dragonfly

Susan, I knew that at some point you would see this envelope leaning against the kettle. You won't hear from me again, but my solicitor will be writing to you. I have enclosed a list of contact numbers you may need. None of these people know where I am, or anything else about me. I'm not even sure that it will really matter to you, except that you will miss not having a housekeeper, cook and chauffeur. You may not know this, but I was recently referred to the local hospital for tests. You may remember I was meeting some old work colleagues for a few days of golf; it was a lie.

The staff were so welcoming and helpful; it made me realise how cold and sterile our relationship has become. I had quite a few tests and had to wait a couple of days for the results. I had found a seat in a small garden with a pond adjoining the ward. It was good weather, and very relaxing. I thought I was alone, but from behind me I heard a sudden intake of breath.

"A dragon-fly! Isn't it beautiful?"

I looked round and discovered it was a nurse from the ward. We watched as the sun lit the creature's flight over the roof.

"I'm sorry, but I have always loved dragon-flies," she blushed.

"Have you? How much do you know about them?" I asked.

"Not much, but the English dragon-fly doesn't live very long, about ten weeks in all. Six of which is as a larva, under water. They live as developed creatures for only a month; that is if birds or spiders don't catch them. They are a powerful symbol to me. Their vibrancy is almost spiritual." She blushed again, which I found very endearing. By the time I talked to her again I had been diagnosed and discharged from the hospital.

I walked towards the main entrance not knowing what to expect. In the department that deals with cancer patients, June, (that's her name) walked towards me accompanied by her daughter.

"Hello John, how nice to see you. How are you doing?" she smiled.

"I'm not too bad, but this is my first visit since I left and I'm slightly apprehensive," I said.

"The staff in the Chemo department are great, and very helpful, they will explain everything very clearly. Can I introduce my daughter Kate to you? Kate, this is the chap I told you about, the one who had to listen to my ramblings about dragon-flies!"

Kate was as friendly as her mother. As we parted June said she hoped we would meet again. She looked like she meant it.

June and I did meet again of course, I think we were meant to. I've not only found June, but now enjoy the company of her grandchildren, a delight I thought I would never have. We were meant to be together, some quirk of fate caused the delay. It still feels strange when I realise that June loves me. I know my life won't last as long as I would wish, but we are very determined to enjoy every day we have together. I feel so alive now, and have even forgiven myself for living too long as if under water, and allowing you to hold me there. Today, two fifty year olds had dragonflies tattooed on their shoulders as a constant reminder of how really to live.

By Chris Lammas

'Write Now' Profiles

Pat Barber

Pat Barber was born in London and has lived and worked for many years in Eastern Europe and in Spain. She has had poetry published in a Spanish magazine and is currently studying for a Batchelor of Arts degree in Literature with the Open University. After the death of her husband she moved back to the UK, and is now living in Frinton on Sea in Essex.

Albertha Braithwaite

The Group occasionally takes on new members, and we were pleased to welcome local resident Albertha quite recently.

The thing that drew her to 'Write Now' was her love of Poetry. She enjoys it as social comment, but also likes to write verse for her granddchildren. The Frinton literary scene has intrigued her for some time, and she has a secret ambition to publish some of her own work. -- Her fellow Writers have encouraged Albertha to also try her hand at prose, and do you know, she's quite good!

Roma Butcher

I have always enjoyed the written word so when my son Simon suggested I join him at a Creative Writing course in November 1999 I went along happily, not actually expecting to begin leading such a colourful life.

Since that day I have committed mayhem and murder with gay abandon, had numerous illicit and interesting affairs, not to mention husbands and assorted offspring.

From our tutor, John Gladwell I learned to appreciate poetry and now enjoy writing verse in its many forms. When he moved on we were all enjoying ourselves too much to scatter and so formed our group 'Write Now.' We read, write, discuss, argue, both giving and receiving advice and criticism. So far no blows have been struck and we have all met with some success.

Simon Butcher

From a City background, I was forced to semi-retire at the age of forty-five, and although I read a lot, I had time only to superficially enjoy a book. Joining a Creative Writing class opened up a whole new world to me; taught me that anyone is capable of some form of writing. Fiction, poetry, ---- anything. Since putting pen to paper I have been an LA detective, a Master Mariner, I have talked to Charles Darwin and been rude to Tony Blair. I work harder than ever now, but make sure I find time to read, as simple words can take you to anywhere in the world, be anyone you want, even a poet. Several short stories of mine have made print, and that best selling novel is never far away, just round the next corner.

Bill Davies

A Founder Member of 'Write Now', Bill is never short of ideas for the Group to try. He attended John Gladwell's class at Soken House soon after retiring to Frinton in 2000 and contracted the 'Writing Bug.' As an amateur 'thesp' and singer he is attracted to the written word! Among other things he writes poetry and short stories for his grandchildren, and draws on his experiences as a Housing Manager for much of his work. Friends and family plague him with poetry commissions (Unpaid!) for various notable events, eg birthdays, weddings, coming of age etc. He loves it! He also co-edits the newsletter of his Amateur Theatre Company.

He had a poem published in the 'Writers Forum' magazine last year, and has written a biography from his father's war diary which is to be published in 2008. Like many of his colleagues he has a novel on the back-burner (which may or may not find its way onto the bookshelves of the reading public)

Pam Harris

Words are in my head, they float around waiting to come out. It has always been like this, unrecognised until joining the Creative Writing course in 1999. As a first member I was slowly encouraged to express on paper my unwritten words. So far many have emerged, the rest are lined up ready to slip through my fingers. I have had successes one of which was winning the Frinton Literary Festival prose competition in 2006. I am 74 now, enjoy what I do in my amateur way, hoping one day to do 'the big one.'

Jack Hopkins

Now, many years into retirement from teaching, I spend a full life in my hobbies. When the sun shines I play golf. When it's wet I rest, read, or enjoy music, but sometimes, when all these hobbies lose their charms, I sit at the computer, flex my fingers and wonder why perspiration is far more evident than inspiration. At such times the Writing Group can sometimes provide the pinprick that stirs me into action and my contributions to this collection are the result of those pinpricks.

Chris Lammas

Born in the Midlands in 1941, Christine later moved to London with her family. She lived there until she retired, having enjoyed a successful career in Health Care. Her final job was to manage a Day Care Centre in Dagenham.

She and husband Bill retired to Walton on the Naze, just over the road from The Triangle shopping centre. Chris had many interests, including painting and pottery. She was a talented singer, one of the interests she shared with Bill, who would accompany her on his guitar. She also loved writing, and joined our group soon after arriving in Walton.

Chris died from cancer on February 4th 2007, leaving Bill and one son. -- She is sadly missed.

Mary-Ann Naicker

Mary Ann was born into a large family in Limerick Eire. At an early age she came to England where she went into

Nursing, and then Social Work. A widow with two sons and two grandchildren she still finds time to write. --- A passion acquired over the years. She came to live in Frinton on Sea four years ago, where she joined 'Write Now.' To date she has had two books published under the name of Penny Davis.

Valerie Woollcott

Valerie joined the Group in Autumn 2006, long after the actual Creative Writing class had ceased. -- She confesses to being an obsessive 'scribbler' and has enjoyed learning from some of the old-stagers. Val is primarily a story-teller. She is equally at home in past or present for her settings, and is sensitive to human emotions and to atmosphere.

The success of the Group is important to Val and she values the friendship that has resulted from sharing ideas and knowledge.

Printed in the United Kingdom
by Lightning Source UK Ltd.
126404UK00001B/58-162/A

9 781434 338648